HIS EARTH MAIDEN

SPACE LORDS: A QURILIXEN WORLD NOVEL

MICHELLE M. PILLOW

MICHELLE M. PILLOW® - MICHELLEPILLOW.COM

His Earth Maiden © copyright 2018 by Michelle M. Pillow

Second Printing July 2018, The Raven Books LLC

First Printing May 2018

ISBN-13: 978-1-62501-419-1

Published by The Raven Books LLC

SPACE LORDS SERIES

His Frost Maiden
His Fire Maiden
His Metal Maiden
His Earth Maiden
His Woodland Maiden

ABOUT HIS EARTH MAIDEN

SPACE LORDS 4

Former elite Federation soldier, now turned space pirate, Jackson Burke has done his best to turn his life around—for the better. He isn't prepared when fate leaves a woman's safety totally in his hands. Since heroes don't leave a damsel in distress—and despite being outlaw pirates, the crew considers themselves the good guys—Jackson assumes responsibility for the beauty. It's enough that his ship is held together by rust and sheer will, now he's got to keep this good guy thing straight and not give in to the urges the sassy female brings out in him. Raisa is everything a man could want and for some reason she seems to like him, rough edges and all, but he's on the Federation's wanted list…and they aren't known to back down.

A Qurilixen World Novel
Space Pirates, Science Fiction Romance

MichellePillow.com

WELCOME TO QURILIXEN

Qurilixen World Novels

Dragon Lords Series
Barbarian Prince
Perfect Prince
Dark Prince
Warrior Prince
His Highness The Duke
The Stubborn Lord
The Reluctant Lord
The Impatient Lord
The Dragon's Queen

Dynasty Lords Series

Seduction of the Phoenix

Temptation of the Butterfly

To learn more about the Qurilixen World series of books and to stay up to date on the latest book list visit www.MichellePillow.com

AUTHOR UPDATES

To stay informed about when a new book is released
sign up for updates:

http://michellepillow.com/author-updates/

organ Black Market
City of Madaga, Planet of Torgan.

There were defining moments in his life when Jackson Burke had known things would never be the same. The day he had been compelled as a young boy living in an orphanage to join the Federation Military—more from a longing for adventure than a sense of galactic duty. The day he was promoted into a secret program to create super soldiers, where he was tested on, trained, and held to the highest of standards. The day he met Captain Jarek and signed on to sail the high skies as a security officer on a pirate ship instead of staying with the Federation, much to the military's disappointment. The day their pilot, Rick, had insulted a vengeful spirit who put a love curse on the heads of five of the crewmen.

And today, the day he decided it was a good day to die.

Death had come calling for him more times than he could count. By all rights, he should have been blown up, or incinerated, or sucked into deep space, or crash landed on some remote planet. Actually, in all those cases, he probably could have blamed Rick. Half the time, the crew couldn't decide if they wanted to save their pilot from trouble or leave his stupid ass behind.

Rick was the reason they were currently stranded on Torgan with a broken ship they couldn't afford to fix.

Bound Virgin wasn't technically their ship. It belonged to Princess Samantha of the Var—the former captain who had kidnapped a shifter prince named Falke and ultimately married him. She wouldn't be happy that her ship was out of commission. Jackson had been sailing the high skies with Falke's brother Jarek at the time of the kidnapping. When Jarek married and settled down, his crew and Samantha's crew had merged. Captain Lochlann and Jackson now flew with Rick, brothers Lucien and Viktor, and Dev. Lochlann's wife, Alexis, and Dev's wife, Violette, also traveled with them.

Jackson guessed none of that history mattered anymore, seeing as he faced the end. Because there was no way in all the blasted space novas he was going back into the Federation Military. There had been a time when he believed in greater causes, but he'd been young and impressionable. At that age, all young men had wanted to believe they were part of a solution. But the Federation wasn't purely good, and their missions were not against evil. Jackson had seen too much corruption in his travels. Yes, the military had its place. The men who served were some of the best he'd ever known. But Jackson felt he'd done his duty. He wasn't going back.

Three young soldiers surrounded him, as if to block him from escape. They had the eager expressions of cadets on their first mission. Jackson could evade them and run, but that would mean putting a target on his back. The inability of the Federation to find him is the only thing that kept them from forcing him back into service. He knew how this would go. The Federation didn't ask. They commanded.

"Soldier J-67114, upon contact, we have orders to detain—"

Jackson lifted his eyes from the ground to look at the young recruit talking to him. That one expression was enough to cut off the man's words. The black uniform was standard issue, without any distinctions of rank or battle. The man looked at his handheld device and swallowed nervously. Jackson crossed his arms over his chest and widened his stance.

The soldier tried again. "We have orders to inform you that you are to be detained for—"

"No," Jackson interrupted.

"What did you say?" The soldier looked confused.

"No," Jackson repeated.

"What do you mean, no?" He looked to his buddies for help.

"The Federation really let their standards slip when they enlisted you, didn't they? No is a word derived from the Old Star language that means you better get out of my way or I'll launch you into deep space."

The soldier glanced up as if Jackson would actually throw him through the glass and metal ceiling of the trading center. It wasn't unusual to run into Federation soldiers on the planet of Torgan, but Jackson tended to avoid them when he could. It was an unspoken understanding that, unless there was a serious threat, the military left the traders who came to the black-market planet alone. Apparently, this was one overly eager recruit who hadn't been given the memo.

The Torgan marketplace kept up the appearance of being a legitimate trading center and made enough space credits to slip money into the hands of all the right officials. Ships from around the galaxies landed on the grayish-brown orb.

From the sky, the planet didn't look like much—a desert of dust and sand which was ill-suited to anything but storing space trash, and whose three rings wrapping the planet's sky were the only hint of natural beauty in the desolate landscape. Despite this, the planet thrived because underneath the adobe-style businesses surrounding the large trading complex, lay a darker purpose. If it was fenced, illegal, tawdry, or sought after, someone on Torgan would have it for sale. If there was a price to be had or a deal to be made, someone would make it and very few questions would be asked. Want someone killed? Ask around the center bar. Need stolen medical supplies? Ask around the docks. Need—

"You're J-67114," the soldier insisted.

Jackson lied. "No."

"But your scan—" The soldier held up his device as if that was infallible evidence.

Jackson grabbed the handheld and threw it against a wall. "Looks broken. You should ask for a new one."

"That's Federation property. By order of the...

the…" The soldier tried to pull his blaster from his waist.

"Run," Jackson ordered under his breath. "Or I'll throw you next. You have no idea what you're getting yourself into."

Jackson felt a blaster press to the small of his back.

He hadn't forgotten the other two. He had just hoped they'd be smart enough to back away from the situation.

He glanced over the docking platform. Ships were lined up in tight formation along the concrete area. No one landed or took off without permission, so even if their ship wasn't broken, he wouldn't be making a fast escape.

"Why don't you go see if the Galaxy Playmates show is about to start?" Jackson suggested. He paused as a group of slender Klennup males walked by in shiny gold suits. When they were out of earshot, he continued, "Forget you saw me. Tell them your handheld was broken in a bar fight. They'll believe it. Bar fights happen about every three minutes—"

"You don't look too tough with a blaster in your back," the soldier behind him jeered.

Jackson caught Rick leaning against a wall near the main complex's entrance. The man was as human as they came, with short brown hair, brown eyes, and the same irritatingly amused expression regardless of the situation. The pilot grinned and made no move to help him. Someone caught Rick's attention, and he motioned them forward.

Dev appeared in the entryway. People were usually terrified of his red skin and black eyes. If that didn't scare a person, then his large size would.

Instead of helping, Dev crossed his arms and nodded once, as if ready for a show. Unless Jackson called out to him, he would not join the fight.

"Last chance to walk away—" Jackson tried to offer.

His words were cut off as a sharp blow hit the back of his head.

Instinct and training kicked in. He swung around, ducking as he maneuvered his elbow into the soldier's stomach. The blaster went flying, but he didn't hear it land against the hard floor. He punched back, making contact with the man's jaw to send him stumbling.

Every fighting move the Federation had taught these men, Jackson had mastered long ago. Every dirty fighting trick they might have, Jackson had probably faced in his years sailing the high skies. It was over before it had started. As the man with the blaster fell, Jackson punched the second man and swept his leg into the knees of the third.

A slow clap sounded as the last man fell. Jackson

straightened and frowned. He hadn't wanted this mess. It was random bad luck that these three had been out scanning for trouble.

Rick clapped, still grinning. Dev held the blaster he'd caught when the first soldier fell.

"Blasted space cadets," Jackson swore.

A large, hairy alien walked past, paused to look at the three fallen men and laughed. The sound rumbled from his chest in low, hard beats. He didn't stop to help. At least that was one thing in Jackson's favor. Not too many Torgan visitors would be bothered by what had happened.

Dev picked up the handheld Jackson had smashed against the wall. He thrust it at Jackson. "Get on the ship and don't come off. I'll send Viktor to see what he can salvage from the data."

"We need space credits," Jackson denied. "I'm supposed to be at the Frendle's Chips table."

Gambling was just one of the ways they were able to earn. Lochlann was trying to sell whatever they didn't need. Rick and Lucien were trying to sell what they'd, um, found abandoned on remote planets. Those items required a special buyer. Viktor sold his services as a mechanic doing repairs on the dock. Though no one told the women, Dev's role was to keep an eye on them and make sure they didn't fall into trouble. Alexis and Violette were capable, but their husbands worried. Jackson found it amusing. He felt sorry for any man who tried to cross those two females.

"Go," Dev ordered.

Jackson could have refused. He was the ship's security officer. But, out of all the crewmen, he'd spent the most time with Dev. They'd fought side by side for hours in the virtual reality training room. He had learned to trust his friend's judgment.

Jackson carried the handheld toward the ship. Seeing the hunk of metal resting useless in its space, he frowned. There was nothing worse for a sailor than being landlocked. The fun of visiting planets and fuel docks was knowing they could always take off the second things became too rough.

It would be a shame if they had to scrap their ship as junk metal. Though it wasn't much to look at, when it was running it was a fine vessel. Previous owners had installed medical units in all the rooms. He wasn't one hundred percent sure of the history —the ship's records were as fake as Rick's pretend girlfriends—but he deduced the ship had belonged to Kintok sex traders at one point. Secret compartments and manacles over beds kind of gave it away.

The ship scanner recognized him and opened as he neared the bottom hatch. He jumped up and pulled himself in through the small opening before the ladder could make its way down. He hit a button, closing himself inside.

The lights running along the walls flickered at half power, but he could find his way around in the dark. An electrical system malfunction had ignited a confined gas pocket, which then destroyed vital parts of the propulsion system. Without it, the ship would chug slowly through the deep black, most likely running out of life support before reaching the next planet. They were lucky to be alive.

Jackson could handle the dark, but it was the silence that bothered him. With the engines off, there was no vibration against his feet. The lights flickered, giving a small buzz as they tried to light his way as sensors detected his presence. He stepped a little louder than normal just to hear the *thud* of his feet on the metal. There were no voices in the cockpit or in the dining hall. There was no music from old transmission waves they'd captured.

He went to the cockpit and sat in the pilot's chair. The Federation device wouldn't turn on, so he set it aside. He doubted it would tell them why the military wanted him back, but maybe Viktor could erase it, break it down and sell off the parts.

Unwilling to sit in the dim light in silence, Jackson pulled up the security feed to watch outside the ship. The lights in the corridor behind him flickered as power was diverted to the screens. He settled back into the pilot's chair and kicked up his feet. A few aliens walked by, the only entertainment as they briefly sauntered past to leave him staring at an empty concrete walkway.

2

Raisa Lovell clawed her way through the dry sand. It covered her skin, sticking to the sweat to rub uncomfortably in some unfortunate areas. She coughed as she inhaled dust. Torgan's temperatures were not the hottest in the universe, but they felt damned close. It was so hot that her attackers had given up digging the shallow grave and just kicked sand over her.

Colleagues had warned her about coming to Torgan, but Raisa was desperate. She needed parts to fix her molecular gastro-spectrometer. If she didn't, she wouldn't be able to send in coding for recipes for the new model of food simulators being manufactured. No recipes meant no space credits, which meant no way to earn over the next few years, which meant she'd starve stranded on some back-planet outpost. Or worse, she'd have to apply for a job with the ESC. The Exploratory Science Commission would assign her to some laboratory, and she'd have no say in the bureaucratic nonsense they would foist on her.

Right now, bureaucratic didn't sound half bad. At least they'd give her something to drink. And come looking for her if she disappeared. At present, no one was looking for her. She was on her own.

She tried to croak out a sound as she passed one of the adobe shops. The man standing in the doorway glared at her suspiciously and shut the door. No one would want to get involved with a dirt-covered humanoid woman. For one, they had no reason to help her. People on Torgan rarely did anything without monetary motivation. For another, self-preservation would tell them to mind their own business. Her best bet was to get to the main trading complex.

The sand slid beneath her feet, making it hard to walk. The breeze stirred the granules until they found their way into every nook. She covered her mouth with her arm and kept her head down.

It felt like an eternity before she reached the modern complex. Metal steps led from the sand to the glass barrier that would let her back inside. Breathing hard, she pulled her herself up by the rail as her legs shook to keep her upright. Her head pressed against the glass and she waved her arm in front of the scanner. It didn't immediately open to let her pass and she had to make several attempts.

When the glass finally slid open, she wasn't ready for it and she fell forward onto her hands and knees. The door slid shut and the ventilation turned on, blowing up from the floor to suck the dirt from her body. The cool breeze was welcome, and she was disappointed when it stopped. She crawled into the complex. The metal floor turned to concrete. She collapsed forward, letting her body soak in the cool.

Raisa had no idea how long she lay on the complex floor, or if she even retained consciousness for that time. Not one person stopped to offer assistance. The universe really was a lonely place.

Her mind raced, as if trying to shock her body into action. She couldn't stay on the floor. She needed to get to the ship she'd commissioned for a ride. She needed to find someone with a part for her...

For the unit they had stolen from her. Her molecular gastro-spectrometer was gone. Without it she couldn't work, and there was no way she was going to find another one.

Raisa wanted to lay down and cry, but the sound of footsteps propelled her into action. She gritted her teeth and jerked her body upright. Her left leg felt numb and tingled each time she put pressure on it. She limped down the concrete walkway, past the rows of ships.

The rough mix of humanoids and other aliens milled around the docking lot. She kept a lookout for the traders who had double crossed her, but really didn't trust anyone she saw. A hairy creature with matted braids all over his body argued with a short green humanoid who had over a dozen tiny horns poking out of the top of his head. They stopped when they saw her. Raisa averted her gaze and held still until they continued on.

Alien creatures didn't frighten her. As strange as they might look to her with their blue skin, or wings, or reptilian flesh, she probably appeared just as odd to them. Her mother, Janice Lovell, had been a human from New Earth, and her father, Harpin, was Angelion. She didn't inherit his wings, but she did have his knack for repairing mechanical and electrical things. Angelions were particularly adept when it came to technology. It's probably why she was so good at figuring out the recipe codes for food simulators.

People said she looked like her mother, though Raisa barely remembered the woman. Janice had been part of a technophobe movement and refused medical treatment for an injury. At five years old, Raisa didn't understand. Later in life, however, it became difficult not to resent the woman for not fighting to survive. It was fairly obvious Janice's rejection of technology had come from her breakup with Harpin. They didn't part on nice terms.

She wondered why she was thinking of her parents. Maybe it was because she had no one else to think about. Jobby Dawks deposited space credits into her account. They always got along, but she wouldn't go so far as to call him a friend. She'd made various contacts around the universes, some she'd even been invited to stay with in their homes as she studied every culinary dish they knew how to make. Food simulators were big business, and the more cultures they could represent with their recipe collections, the more units they could sell.

Why was she thinking about work? Raisa touched her head, and realized she was leaning against a metal hull for support. Beneath a layer of sand on her forehead was a sticky substance. She pulled her fingers away and saw blood. A hot tear slid down her cheek. She swiped it with the back of her hand. She did not want to be here, alone, on a dangerous outpost filled with criminals. There was always a risk when she landed at a new location, but this was what her mother would have called the fallen angel's playground.

She forced her feet to move. *One step. Drag a foot. Two steps. Drag a foot. Three…*

Raisa stumbled. Kod and Dak hadn't bothered to make a run for it after leaving her for dead. She found them in the docking lot, standing near the bag that contained her molecular gastro-spectrometer. She would have guessed them to be brothers. They had the same look to them—not just the shape of their green faces and oval bald heads, but the way they carried themselves. Each had a way of opening their mouths ever so slightly at the corner after finishing a sentence. This had been her first encounter with their kind, and she didn't know what manner of aliens they were.

Anger filled her, temporarily erasing the pain as she focused on that bag. She wasn't about to let them keep it. Raisa backed away until she was just out of sight and crossed the narrow walkway to the next row of docked ships. She ducked beneath them, limping from one metal protrusion to another. As she neared the brothers, she leaned down onto all fours and crept forward. The bag was in sight.

Raisa crawled forward. The pain in her leg couldn't be ignored each time she put pressure on her knee. The belly of a ship came too low and she had to stretch onto her stomach. All she had to do was slither forward on the floor and grab the bag while they were deep in conversation. She reached her hand forward and dug her toes into the ground to inch closer.

Almost…almost…almost…almo—got it!

Raisa hooked her finger on a strap and began to pull.

The sound of the bag sliding against concrete caught the brothers' attention, and they both turned to look at her. Disbelief registered on their faces. Dak made an awful sound, a cross between a scream and a growl.

Raisa held the bag tight and tried to thrust herself back. But with the weight of the bag, her awkward position beneath the ship, and her beaten body, it was difficult to move.

As Dak's fist came barreling down toward her head, someone grabbed hold of her ankle and pulled.

She cried out in surprise as she slid out of Dak's reach. The bag skidded with her. She passed beneath a pair of spread legs. A man placed himself between her and the attackers. From what she saw from her place on the floor, he had long dark blond hair and broad shoulders. The skin on the back of his arm looked to be human.

Kod and Dak ran around the side of the ship. She knew first hand that they had fists like lead hammers. Dak punched and the man artfully leaned to the side. The blow missed its mark, darting past the man's head. Before Dak could pull his arm back, the man grabbed his wrist and flung his arm to the side.

Dak spun under the force of the push, and his fist made contact with his brother's nose. Kod screamed in pain as he fell back before covering his bloodied face.

Raisa pushed up from the ground as Dak charged the man. She gave a small cry of exertion as she swung the bag along the floor at Dak's feet. The molecular gastro-spectrometer hit the man's ankles.

Dak lost his footing, flung to the side, and hit his head on a ship. The loud *thud* reverberated around them. He collapsed on the floor.

Amidst the strange screeching cry of Kod, she tried to pull her bag closer. Her muscles trembled. She couldn't force herself to stand.

"Come with me," her rescuer ordered.

Raisa looked up at him.

"On your feet," he said, the tone both commanding and urgent as he glanced around.

She tried. She really did. Adrenaline and self-preservation could only take a body so far, and she had hit her limit.

He grunted, and she wasn't sure if he was annoyed or disappointed as he leaned over. She held up her hand, thinking he meant to pull her to her feet. Instead, he grabbed her wrist and used it to propel her over his shoulder. He held her steady with one hand and grabbed her bag with the other. The press of a muscular shoulder to her stomach was far from pleasant as he jogged across the docking lot to another row of ships.

By this point, she had no protests left in her. Raisa hung limp, fighting to hold on to her conscious mind before finally giving in to the pain. Her vision dimmed as she watched the backs of his legs.

3

What in the star blazes had he done?

Jackson knew leaving the ship was a bad idea. The Federation guys would be out looking for him. He needed to stay off their radar. Instead, he'd followed a crazed woman around the docking lot and brawled with Dokka traders. The fight had attracted attention, and he had no choice but to grab the woman and run. He carried her past his ship across the lot, circled around, and then slipped back when no one was looking.

By the time he lowered the steps and carried her inside the dimly lit hatch, he realized she'd passed out. He set her bag in the passageway and carried her to the captain's quarters. Lochlann would have to forgive him for laying a dirty lady on his bed, but he needed the built-in ship medical units to take a look at her. With power diverted, the medical booth wouldn't be operating at full capacity, if at all.

"Computer, activate personal medic," Jackson ordered.

"Yes, Grumpy Warrior," the computer answered in a neutral tone.

Jackson grimaced. Viktor was up to his old tricks. The man liked to randomly program the computer response systems when he was bored. Before this, he'd been "The Amazing Space Cadet," which wasn't exactly a compliment since "space cadet" basically meant "newbie idiot." Before that, it had been "Comet Kisser." Wait, no—"Lord Not-Gettin'-Lady-Action."

A light buzz indicated that the medic was working. A mechanical arm lowered from an opening in the ceiling. The unit could normally be accessed from anywhere in the ship, but the current power supply made this room the most likely to work. Plus, it had a comfortable bed, which seemed better for a woman than the crewman quarters he had.

The room had manacles hanging over the back of the bed and a cage constructed in the middle of the floor. He didn't like to think of what might have gone on here before the ship had found its way to them. Ships were too expensive and hard to come by, so they couldn't exactly be picky. Why else would there be a personal medic that went to every room? It would have been costly to install the extra resources needed to run the unit. Normally ships only needed a medical booth.

The arm went to him first and flashed a light at him.

"Computer, scan subject on the bed."

"Yes, Grumpy Warrior."

Jackson had seen people come in from outside the complex, but rarely were they as grimy as the woman on the bed. She was filthy, covered in a layer of dirt. When she'd passed by the security feed, he'd watched her more out of boredom than concern.

He tried to see past the layer caked on her skin. There was something appealing about her face that caused him to stare. Her hair was dark and fell to her shoulders. His gaze passed over the slope of her nose to parted lips. He had seen much beauty in his travels, enough to know that there was not one definition of perfection. Beauty was fleeting, and he had never put much stock in it. When he'd gone out on military ops, he'd seen some of the most physically beautiful people do some truly horrible things. And he had met creatures that some people thought were too hard to look at who had the gentlest hearts.

What kind of creature was this woman he'd saved? She'd clearly been up to no good as she sneaked in to steal from the traders. So why had he risked the Federation finding him for a thief?

Jackson laughed at himself. That was like the black hole calling deep space dark, or the space pirate calling a thief an outlaw. He was hardly innocent in the ways of petty crime.

He watched the mechanical arm move so lasers could scan the motionless woman. The light danced over her face and neck before skimming over a dusty long-sleeve shirt. The material was dark and clung to her skin. A pair of turquoise overalls covered her chest and legs. The color wasn't exactly stealthy. He wasn't sure what she'd been thinking when she'd tried to steal the bag.

"Report," the computer voice droned. "Medic shows three fractured ribs, bruising along the torso, foreign obstructions in the lungs, scraped skin, dehydration, extreme sun exposure, and twenty-three minor cuts. Would you like to proceed with treatment, Grumpy Warrior?"

"Yes." Jackson frowned. He knew she hadn't been banged up that badly in the fight. Had his run around the docking lot caused fractured bones and bruises? Being gentle hadn't been his main concern at the time, but he hadn't tossed her around that hard.

The mechanical arm lowered itself beside her face and a long needle extended to pierce her neck. The succession of light hissing sounds indicated that medicine was being pushed through as it injected her with multiple substances. He trusted the unit to do its job, so he didn't bother to ask what the computer was giving her. The needle retracted.

"Medical booth required for further treatment of internal injuries. Please restore power and proceed to the booth at once, Grumpy Warrior."

"Computer, is she in pain?" Jackson asked.

"Analysis of nervous system indicates she is, Grumpy Warrior."

"Can you help that?" he inquired.

"Yes, Grumpy Warrior."

"Do it," he ordered.

"Yes, Grumpy Warrior." The arm realigned itself on the opposite side of her neck and pierced her skin a second time to inject her.

"And kill Viktor while you're at it for making you annoying," Jackson grumbled.

"I'm sorry but murdering registered crew members is not in my protocol," the computer said, and Jackson moved his lips to mimic her. This wasn't the first time he'd made the request. "Your request is being reported to the ship captain for possible disciplinary action. Please stand by, Grumpy Warrior."

The woman moaned and stirred on the bed. Her eyes opened briefly. They were a deep brown with large green flecks. She blinked once and then closed her eyes. He watched but she didn't move again.

"Jack!" The sound of footsteps punctuated Captain Lochlann's cry. Out of all the crewmen, Jackson had sailed the high skies with Lochlann the longest.

Jackson hurried out of the room to see what was happening. The lights flickered, and he felt the vibration signifying that the engine tried to start. "I'm here."

Lochlann slid to a stop by his door, not even seeming to register that Jackson had been in his room. The captain looked like a human, but in his search, his eyes had shifted to a bright yellow, giving away the fact he was a dragonshifter. The yellow was a sure sign he'd been using his enhanced senses. "Those Federation guys you beat up have called for reinforcements. They're sending more men to try to apprehend you. Viktor found a part that should get us up and running. We won't be the fastest ship, but if we leave now we should be able to get you out of here before they arrive."

"What about the supplies? The medical booth's cartridges need to be restocked, and we need to be able to do more than limp along in the deep black." Jackson would die before he went back, but that didn't mean he'd let this crew—*his family*—fly into an uncertain sky.

"We'll figure it out," Lochlann said. "I need you to go to the cargo hold with Dev to unload the heavy equipment. Rick and Lucien found buyers. Cover your face before you go. Do your best to stay out of sight."

"If we have a major accident, there won't be enough medicine to cover the—"

"That's an order," Lochlann said, cutting him off. "I heard your protest, Jackson, but I don't give a flying saucer. A threat to you is a threat to us. We'll figure the rest out from the sky. Go help Dev. Hurry."

Jackson didn't answer but hurried toward the cargo hold. Every little bit of weight they dropped helped. Dev already had a pile started near the hatch of supposed items to be sold. He'd also pushed a large crate as far as he could, which was only a few feet from the wall.

"Loch sent me to help."

"I need that cargo we scavenged on Sintaz," Dev said.

"The lab equipment?" Jackson began looking around for a crate.

"No, the snow suits," Dev said.

"Really, the suits?" Jackson asked in surprise. "We use those."

"Not anymore," Dev said. "No cold landings for us for a while. It's either snow suits or a working secondary generator."

"They're over here." Jackson went to gather the suits. "I compression packed them behind the load of circuits we found in the Zonar District." He tossed a small disc of vacuum-sealed clothing toward Dev. The man caught it easily. Jackson continued to toss the clothing discs until they were all added to the stack.

"Now all I need are the crystals we liberated from Fajerk, the fractal hypnosis disc—"

"And are you serious? We finally unloaded the fractal disc?" Jackson was surprised. They'd carried that thing around since he'd first joined up with his current crew.

"Some Corge thinks it's pretty." Dev took a box off a stack and moved it aside. "And with that, we should have everything Viktor needs to get us into space."

"You mean limp into space," Jackson corrected.

"We've flown with worse," Dev reminded him, not appearing concerned. "This is the life we chose. This is the life we live."

Jackson knew the man wanted to mean it, but

things had changed with Dev since he'd fallen in love. Violette could well take care of herself, but that didn't stop her husband from worrying. Jackson couldn't blame his friend. As a half Bevlon, half human, Dev had a hard hand dealt to him in life. He was cursed as a demon by humans, and the Bevlon looked at him as weak. Violette was a well-deserved bright spot.

"You know it's not the same as it was. When it was just the crew, yes, it's true we all knew what we signed up for. But you have Violette to think about now. Lochlann has Alexis. I won't have their lives risked for—"

"Did you just say I wasn't a member of this crew?" Violette Craven Stephans' voice carried with it a familiar wryness. She was a beautiful woman with vivid green eyes that were always full of mischief. Her words were often clipped short but always sounded secretive, if not a little mocking.

"What, no," Jackson tried to backtrack. "You're a woman and—"

"Thanks for noticing," Violette inserted. "But I already broke Dev's curse. I'm not doing yours as well."

"Wh-what? No, I didn't mean…" Jackson tried to explain. "I know you're the fire element with Dev."

Rick had insulted an ancient spirit, Zhang An,

and she'd cursed the five crewmen present at the time to find love within one of the five Lintianese elements—water, earth, fire, metal and wood. One element for each crewmember. If they didn't recognize their sign, they'd be forever alone.

Evan, who was now settled on the same planet as Captain Samantha, had found Josselyn encased in stone on an ice planet. So she was clearly earth or frozen water. Dev was obviously fire with his demonic heritage. That one was easy. Lochlann had thought Alexis was a droid when they'd first met, so she could be metal. But then, they had also crash landed a ship at the time, nearly running out of oxygen, so that could mean she was connected to earth.

So what was left? Maybe wood. Maybe water. Maybe earth. Maybe metal.

In truth, Jackson hated thinking about it. There was no deciphering the vague clue. He wasn't sure he wanted to fall in love. Companionship would be nice, but he realized the odds of a man like him settling down were not great.

He thought of the woman lying in the captain's quarters. She would make a nice companion. Of course, he was judging that wholly on how he imagined she might be once she woke up and washed off the dirt.

"Did you hit your head? I'm a little worried about you, Jackson," Violette teased.

Jackson again attempted to explain what he'd been saying. "You married Dev—"

"You're stating the obvious." Violette walked across the cargo hold to her husband. She lifted up on her toes to kiss him and her hand grazed Dev's neck. He saw the scar that ran down her forearm, but she never talked about how it happened.

"Hello, my star," Dev whispered.

"You married Dev, so you inherited this ship and crew, you didn't sign up for it," Jackson inserted quickly before the woman could interrupt.

"I'm going to pretend the Federation guys hit you in the head and forget you said that," Violette stated. "Because I know you didn't just say I wasn't as invested in this life as the rest of you."

"I didn't—" Jackson threw up his hands. "Think what you want, woman."

"He means to protect you," Dev said, finally trying to help his friend out. "He means no offense."

"*Sacre!*" Violette swore under her breath before saying, "Then he needs to stop acting like the women on this ship are delicate rays of sunshine in need of saving from their shadows. I earned my place in the deep black. I captained a ship full of ruffians."

"What's riled you up?" Alexis appeared in the doorway, as if by some fortuitous bad luck timing.

"Nothing," Jackson said, suppressing a groan. "Dev, come on, let's get this heavy cargo out of here."

"Why just Dev? Don't you think girls can help carry boxes?" Violette asked.

Jackson tucked his head and moved to a crate. He wasn't going to answer. The weight of the cargo would take all of his and Dev's strength combined, and even then, they'd have to slide it down the loading plank to the floor.

Dev laughed. "Leave the poor man be, my love."

"Fine," Violette said, her voice instantly changing to playful. "Jackson, I'm teasing you. I know what you meant. I also know that not one of us questions the decision to get you out of here."

Jackson breathed a little easier.

"Dev, Lochlann wanted me to tell you that we should be up in the air in about an hour," said Alexis. "I accessed the records from the ship, and I think Viktor and I have come up with a work-around. But it means the comms will be down as we divert power to the life support systems, so he'll need you to come to the cockpit the minute the cargo is delivered and the hatch is fully secured for takeoff."

Dev nodded and made a gruff sound of agreement.

Alexis tried to leave, but Jackson stopped her. "What about the medical booth? Will it be functional?"

Alexis arched a brow and looked him over. Finally, as if deciding there was no pressing reason as to why he'd asked, she relaxed a little. "I'll see what I can do. I have to work on the life support systems first, but I can probably get it up and running sometime after takeoff."

Jackson nodded in understanding. That would have to do. Alexis left.

"Jackson, if you can get the bulk down the hatch, I'll help Dev deliver it. There's no need for you to be seen outside." Violette reached for a handheld device her husband carried and read the list of sold items to herself. She looked around the cargo hold before saying, "The fractal hypnosis disc is tucked behind the ESC food packs. We had to hide it from Lucien. He kept trying to hypnotize his brother."

Violette kissed her husband one more time before going to retrieve the item.

Jackson thought of the woman passed out on the captain's bed. He wasn't sure why he didn't mention her to his friends. They wouldn't be happy that he went outside and risked exposure, but that wasn't it. If he were honest with himself, he didn't want them to make her leave. He wasn't sure what was going on with the Dokka traders, and she was in no condition to defend herself if he dumped her unconscious body on the docking lot and left her.

4

Raisa pried open an eye and stared at the metal ceiling. A blurry object hovered close to her face and she tried to push away from it. She lay on her back. The comfortable mattress pressed against her, and she found it difficult to slide across it. The object followed her, and she felt a prick against her neck.

Automatically, she flung an arm up to stop whatever it was, and the back of her knuckles struck metal. The device pulled away and she was able to see a needle retracting inside a mechanical holder.

A burning sensation flowed from her neck down the side of her body, leaving numbness in its wake. The medical unit didn't scare her as much as the unknown reason behind it. She remembered the man helping her and was grateful, but she wasn't exactly sure what he expected from her in return. Tilting her head to look around, her gaze fell on the manacles hanging on the wall behind her.

Raisa sat up, weaving as she tried to work her way toward the edge of the bed. A cage in the middle of the room caught her attention next. A sick feeling washed over her. Suddenly, her rescuer wasn't appearing so heroic. She should have known better than to go to Torgan.

She swayed. This wasn't like walking through the dusty hell of Torgan's landscape. Though warm, the air wasn't oppressive in the ship. She went toward the door and pressed her ear against the cooler metal to listen. The slight hum of the electronics spoke to her Angelion senses and she lifted her hand to where the door scanner appeared to be. Without looking, she followed her instincts to open the door. She heard the scanner engage, as if the unit spoke a secret language she could understand.

As the door began to slide upward, she moved out of the way.

Suddenly, the door stopped with a loud *clank* and the lights flickered before shutting off. Instant darkness surrounded her as each sensor light died.

Raisa held very still and tried to stifle the sound of her rapid breathing. Was someone coming for her? Why had they shut off the lights? Nothing about this could be good.

Her hands shook as she felt her way down the frozen door to find the space beneath. It had opened just enough for her to squeeze through to the other side. Instinct told her that she needed to try.

Raisa inched down onto the floor and used what weak strength she could muster to pull herself under the narrow opening. She moved her hands over her head and pushed against the outside wall. Whatever the machine had injected into her took away sensation. She felt the metal, but it was more like an impression or a memory and not the work of her nerve endings.

Her eyes felt heavy and she let them close. It was dark anyway and she couldn't see anything. She edged under the door, pushing with all her might.

Push harder. Harder. Come on, Raisa, move your...

5

Jackson ran his hand against the wall in the darkness as he made his way back toward the captain's quarters. Power was fluctuating all over the ship, and Viktor had diverted energy from all nonessential systems for takeoff. That included the lights. They were literally flying in the dark as Rick guided the ship off planet.

He stumbled as the ship lurched. Technically, he should have been strapped into a seat, but he wanted to check on the woman he'd rescued. He'd left her on the bed. With the gravitational controls not stabilizing the inside of the ship, Jackson worried she would be unconscious and bouncing dangerously all over the room.

Jackson heard footsteps coming toward him and realized whoever was there probably hadn't heard him. He had a natural stealth that was hard to turn off. He consciously made noise by heavying his steps.

"Who is that?" a female whispered.

"Alexis?" Jackson asked. "What are you doing in the passageways? You're supposed to be in the cockpit."

"It took me a moment to process the right information, but I think I might be able to figure out the wiring for the lights. They don't match this ship's official schematics at all." Alexis had been used as a test subject by a corporation that manufactured pleasure droids. They uploaded files into her brain and used her as a base model to create lifelike companions.

"That's good." Jackson wasn't sure how much was stored in her brain, but he'd heard Lucien estimate there were millions of files, from ship schematics to biomedicine to books by famous authors. Humans weren't meant to carry so much knowledge, and what was left after the experiments was a living computer database. At one point she'd been connected to the Pleasure Droid Corporation mainframe, but that connection was severed to protect her from capture. It sometimes took her a while to sort through the information, but she almost always came through. She'd even saved Jackson's life once when a shipwreck had left him with a knife blade lodged in his side.

"We'll see if it works." She sounded frustrated. "Some of it is Viktor's modifications. Some of the wire patterns resemble a few known samples of smuggler ships caught by the Federation over the years, which means there are probably secret holds none of you has even seen on this thing. Others look to be official HIA mods, which honestly, I don't want to know how you guys got hold of those."

"That doesn't explain what you're doing running around in the dark. You should be somewhere safe," Jackson said.

Alexis laughed in dismissal. "Violette was right. You *are* feeling overprotective today. I—*ow!*"

Alexis stumbled, and he followed the sounds she made to catch her before she fell.

"Blasted Rick," Jackson swore. "The wires will have to wait. The ship isn't steady and—"

"What the hell was that?" Alexis pushed away from him.

The vibration of the ship changed, becoming lighter as they entered deep space. The lights flickered and turned on. He looked down to where Alexis was sweeping her hand over the floor. She gasped and pulled back.

"What in the blazing star trails?" Alexis swore under her breath. "Where did she come from?"

The woman he'd rescued lay on the floor beneath the door. Her head and one hand stuck into the passageway, face down. It looked as if she'd been trying to crawl out of the room.

He knelt beside her. "I rescued her and didn't know where else to put her."

"You kidnapped a—"

"*Rescued*," Jackson stressed.

The lights flickered again. A hissing sound came from the door. He shared a look with Alexis. They both grabbed an arm and jerked the woman into the passageway. The door reset itself and slid shut, barely missing her feet. The woman landed partly on his lap. Jackson uncomfortably adjusted his hips and moved out from under her.

"Jackson, why were you hiding this stranger on board? Who is she?" Alexis leaned over to examine the woman's head with a worried look.

"She needed help." The answer was simple, but it was the only truth he knew to tell.

"Why didn't you say anything before takeoff?" Alexis stroked back the woman's hair to reveal the side of her face. "I don't think I kicked her too hard when I tripped on her head, but it's hard to tell under all this dirt. I'm more worried about her neck."

"We need this ship back to full power," Jackson

said in irritation. "The safety mechanisms should have engaged. She could have been crushed."

Alexis arched a brow but clearly chose to ignore is grumpy tone. "What happened to her?"

"I'm not entirely sure. I found her in the docking lot." He didn't feel the need to mention she was stealing at the time, not that anyone on the ship would care about that little fact. "I had the medical unit in your room examine her and it said she was dehydrated and had three fractured ribs." Jackson supported her head. "Help me turn her over."

Alexis helped roll the woman onto her back to make her more comfortable. Dust covered her in patches, dirtying her face and clothes. Jackson stared at her face, willing her eyes to open and knowing it was best if they didn't. A fractured rib would be excruciatingly painful. How had she not screamed in agony as he ran through the docking lot with her?

"She's the reason why you kept saying we needed to restock the medical booth before we took off." It was more a statement than a question. "I wish you had told me. We had to divert power away from the medical booth. It was a calculated risk. It was either that or our food supply. We choose to keep the food simulator running."

"We need to help her. I had the medic give her something for pain. I don't know how she made it to the door, but she shouldn't have been able to get up and walk."

"We might be at the tail end of the pain medicine cartridges. They're probably not at full potency." Alexis sighed heavily. "I kept telling you guys to take your hangovers like men."

Jackson ignored the jibe. He slipped his arms beneath the woman's body and lifted her off the floor. Her slight figure worried him, and he tried not to put pressure on her rib cage while supporting her head. "Can you access one of your head file things and see if you can help her?"

"Sure. I'll access my head file things. For the record, I prefer to call it a database." Alexis looked at him thoughtfully. "But why do you need *me* to look it up? Didn't they give you field medicine training in the military? I thought you were some kind of super soldier. Surely you've come across worse injuries than this."

"None of my missions involved rescue orders." Jackson didn't like thinking about the past, let alone talking about it. "If we were injured, we had an injector to keep us going until we reached the base."

Alexis gave him a contemplative smile. "Do you think she's the one to break your curse?"

"No," Jackson instantly denied. "I think the true curse is the *threat* of the curse. It makes us overthink each situation, each woman we come across. When you think of how many stops we've made all over the universe, how many women we've crossed paths with, the odds are not in our favor."

"Lochlann told me what Zhang An said." Alexis' eyes glazed and she stared forward. He knew she was accessing the memory. She spoke the words the spirit had use to curse them, "Together you travel and together you'll remain. Tied and joined like the five elements of our people."

"The road to happiness is very rocky for all of you." Jackson finished the ghost's curse. He didn't need Alexis to tell him the rest. He remembered every word. Zhang An had gone on to say, *"You will find your love hidden within the mysteries of the five elements. One element for each of you. The corresponding element will hold the secret to your future happiness. But fate is not clear. If you do not recognize it, you will lose it and be forever alone."*

Five elements. Five men. Simple as far as curses went.

And yet very complicated.

"Three of the five found happiness. I consider that a success. Lochlann, Dev, and Evan were the most deserving out of all of us." Jackson found it hard to feel sorry for the pilot. It was Rick's fault they had been cursed to begin with.

"Don't you think you deserve happiness?" Alexis

placed a hand on his arm, and he leaned away from her touch.

Jackson tried to activate the door scanner to the captain's quarters without jostling the woman he carried. Alexis ran her hand over it for him. He hadn't bothered to ask permission to put their new guest in the room. He already knew what Alexis' answer would be. Everyone on the crew has a soft spot for an underdog, and what was a battered woman if not in need of their help? They both watched the door inch up slower than normal. He paused briefly before quickly ducking under it, in case the metal slab decided to drop shut again.

"I think she must have been outside," Alexis said. "She's the color of Torgan dirt."

Jackson nodded. He'd thought as much too. "The computer said dehydration, extreme sun exposure, and foreign obstructions in the lungs. I think she breathed in the dust."

"You were right to bring her on board," Alexis said. "I can think of no good reason why a woman would be in the Torgan outdoor markets with sand in her lungs, a beat-up body, and without adequate water."

Jackson laid the woman on the bed, still dusty from the last time he'd put her there. "Do your database thing."

Alexis took a deep breath and began to mumble

to herself as she searched for answers. It was almost as if her other senses shut down when she searched. Her eyes became glazed and distant. Her voice took on a droning quality. "Human anatomy. Skeletal System. Rib cage provides protection to the heart and lungs. Irrelevant to the situation. Reexamine."

Lochlann had explained that her mind worked like a giant database of linked computers, in which she had to follow the pathways until she reached the right information.

"Federation Military guide to field medicine during the Ven wars. Winged creatures. Irrelevant to the situation. Reexamine. Federation Military guide to pre-medic care. Blaster injuries. Crash landings. Fire injury. Protrusions. Fractures. Relevant to the situation. Spiral fracture. Impacted fracture. Transverse fracture. Epiphyseal fracture. Closed fracture. Complete fracture. Broken ribs can move inside the body and puncture organs. Compression can alleviate pain. Compression may cause other problems. Relevant to the situation. Recommended treatment is to use a medical booth. If no medical booth is available—"

"Yes, that one," Jackson interrupted, his words insistent. "Relevant. *Relevant.*"

Alexis' eyes darted to him and her words stuttered as if he made her lose her place. "Re-relevant to situation."

She stopped talking.

"Well?" Jackson asked, ready to help the woman on the bed. "How do we fix it?"

"We can't." Alexis frowned. "All we can do is hope they're not complete factures and keep her still until we can get to a medical booth. They have to heal on their own. She'll have to stay here for now. I don't want to move her again. If it hurts when she coughs or speaks, she can apply a little pressure to the area, but not much. And let her have whatever is left of the pain medicine. When it's out, we're going to have to resort to liquor." She walked to the door. "I'll let Lochlann know we've been kicked out of our room. We'll take yours. You get the rec room."

"Wait, what about her?" Jackson asked. "Shouldn't you stay and…" He gestured helplessly at the woman.

"Do I look like a nursemaid?" Alexis chuckled. "You found her, you take care of her. I have a ship to fix."

"What's a nursemaid?" Jackson frowned.

"You are." Alexis winked before hurrying under the door. "Take care of your patient."

6

R aisa felt as if someone watched her before she even opened her eyes. She stayed in self-imposed darkness, not moving as she listened to the room around her. She thought she heard breathing, but it was more of an awareness than an actual sound. Her body was numb, and she felt an intense heat where she was trying to heal herself.

Finally, she opened her eyes. Green eyes stared back at her from about three inches above her face. She gasped as she tried to push away, back into the mattress.

"You're alive." The man sat back on the bed. Their bodies didn't touch, and he made no other movements as he stared at her.

She glanced at the room several times to get a

sense of where she was without taking her eyes off him for too long. By the metal walls and scanners, it was clear she was on a ship in a luxury suite. The manacles she'd seen behind her earlier where disconcerting, as was the cage. A door led to what looked to be decontaminator shower. The room seemed to turn a corner and she couldn't see the rest.

She didn't know what to say as she tried to reason what was going on. She recognized him from the docking lot and remembered waking up on his ship. He had a handsome face, strong features. Stubble darkened a sculpted jaw, framing firm lips that neither smiled nor frowned. Even with clothes on, she could see the definition of muscles beneath the black shirt. His dark blond hair was long, pulled back behind his neck. She wondered if the hairstyle was a little rebellious, as he had fought like he was trained elite military.

Fight.

Her bag!

She tried to push up on the bed and look around. "My molecular gastro-spectrometer. Where is it? I need it."

He furrowed his brow as he placed a hand on her shoulder to stop her from getting up. The restraint didn't seem to take much effort on his part. He eased her back on the bed, his dark gaze full of warning that she was not to try moving again. "Your ribs are fractured. You must not move around until they're more fully healed or until we find you a working medical booth."

"I need my molecular gastro-spectrometer," she insisted.

"I don't know what that is." He again stopped her from getting off the bed. He glanced at the manacles, as if considering them, but in the end, he simply rested his hand on her shoulder. When she stopped wiggling, he lifted it, extended his fingers and hovered his hand over her for a few moments, as if to make sure she was done trying to leave.

Raisa closed her eyes in frustration. "My bag. Those spaceholes on the dock stole it and tried to bury me in the Torgan wasteland. I need it back. Everything I have is tied to that device."

"It sounds very important."

"It is," she assured him. "Please, tell me you have it."

"I have it," he obliged.

Raisa breathed easier. "Oh, thank goodness. I don't know what I would have done if I had lost it."

"Are you in pain?" he asked.

Raisa reached her hand to where heat focused in her torso. "It's getting better."

"I'm sorry I ran with you over my shoulder. I should have realized you were delicate and would break easily. You must have passed out from the pain." He hung his head and his eyes moved down.

"It's fine." She dismissed his concern. "They must have fractured my ribs when they kicked me after going back on our deal for parts. You had nothing to do with it."

"The Dokka traders kicked you?

"So, can I have it?" she insisted.

"Have what?"

"My molecular gastro-spectrometer." Raisa wanted to see if those two pieces of liger dung had broken anything else on it. Then, realizing that she didn't know this man and he might try to steal it for himself, she added, "It's not valuable or anything. I need it for work."

"It is safe in the cargo hold." The overhead lights blinked, causing him to pause. "We're having a little bit of an issue with our lights." A tremor worked a wave across the ship, shaking the bed. "And the power grid. But don't worry, we're perfectly safe, just limping a little."

"Space," she said in realization. Her mind seemed to clear with each passing second, as the injection they gave her lost effectiveness. "We're in deep space, aren't we?" She didn't wait for his answer as she began to panic. Her eyes went to the manacles over the bed. "Where are you taking me? Where are we? What is this place?"

"This is a ship. We *are* in space, as you said, and we're currently on course for a fueling dock, where we hope to trade for parts to fix our nonessential support systems."

"Oh my stars, you're a cyborg," she blurted as she realized what she was dealing with. That made sense—his blank expression, the fact he had more muscles than almost every human man she'd ever seen, his fighting skills, his matter-of-fact answers, the unyielding way he carried himself as if on alert.

She reached for his face but was unable to touch it from where she lay on the bed, so she touched his chest instead. Warmth spread over her fingers, and she detected a heart beating beneath her palm. She also felt the mechanics inside him, they spoke to her Angelion side, small tickles letting her know they were there and functioning.

He looked down to where her hand rested on him and didn't move.

She pressed her fingers gently against his shirt. She rubbed the flesh and hard muscles beneath, sliding her fingers over the definition of his chest and ribs. "I didn't know they made you this advanced. I couldn't even tell."

He cleared his throat. "I'm not a cyborg."

"But…?" She met his eyes—and realized she'd made a mistake. There may be some mechanics in him, but not enough to make him a hybrid born in a laboratory. He was all male. She snatched her hand away but her fingers tingled as his warmth stayed with her. "Whoa, that injection must have been strong. My head is—"

"The injections are most likely diluted. I'm sorry to say our medical supplies are running low," he stated.

"Couldn't just let me have that one, could you?" she quipped with a small laugh.

"No, I *did* order the medic to give you a full dose, but it must have flushed it with saline to get it through the lines to administer. I want you to have it for your pain, but we're not sure how much is left in the cartridge and—"

"I meant you couldn't let me have the excuse for feeling you up just now," she broke in. "Are you always this serious?"

"No, well, ah…" He sighed. "Yes. Probably."

"Save your pain medication since you're on ration. I'll be fine in a few days," she said. "And in case I didn't say it, thank you for your assistance on the docking lot."

"You could have internal injuries. The computer detected fractures and…" His words trailed off as she reached for her shoulder to unfasten the turquoise overall strap. His eyes watched her fingers move.

"Here, help me pull this down." She flipped the

front flap of the overalls off her chest and tried to push the material down so she could reach the hem of her shirt. It caught on her hips. When he continued to stare, she added, "Please."

He suddenly stood and backed away. "I'm sorry if I gave you the wrong impression. No one on this ship expects payment in the form of," he hesitated, "relations."

"Glad to hear it, as I wasn't offering sex." She managed to unfasten the lock button on her side and reach beneath the material to pull her shirt up to examine the damage done to her stomach. A light blue healing bruise had formed on her skin where they'd struck her.

"What is that?" the man asked. "I have never seen a bruise quite that color of blue." He rushed to the door, slapping his hand against the scanner in his haste to get it open. "Alexis!" he yelled before the metal had even slid up fully.

"It's fine," Raisa said, pushing up from the bed now that he wasn't right beside her to force her to lay down. She kicked the coveralls off her legs and stood in the skin-tight cloth pants she always wore underneath. She took the opportunity to stretch her arms over her head. She winced at the pain it caused and instantly regretted the action. "It's what happens when my body is healing itself."

"You need to lay down," the man insisted. "You can do light pressure, but not too much."

She looked at the bed. She could practically see the outline of her body in the dirt she'd left behind. She studied her dirty hands and frowned as she remembered clawing her way out of a grave. "Uh, actually, it looks like I need a bath."

Raisa wobbled on her feet as the reality of what she'd been through hit her. She'd been dragged out to the barren wasteland and left for dead. It was thanks to the sheer laziness of her attackers that she managed to crawl out of the shallow hole. She could have died. And for what? A part to fix her molecular gastro-spectrometer?

"Bravon's fire, woman," he swore under his breath as he rushed to catch her. She had regained her footing so the rescue wasn't necessary. That didn't stop him from holding her. "Are you always this hardheaded?"

"No," she automatically answered. "Well, actually, yeah, I probably am."

Her body pressed into his as he held her lightly against him. The heat from his body seeped into her skin and she found herself wanting to press closer. It had been a long time since she'd been alone with a man, intimately like this. Well, truth be told, she'd never been alone with a man who looked like him. Part of her wanted to lift up on her toes and kiss him, just once to see what it would be like.

"You might as well call me Raisa," she said, "after all we're in deep space together."

She wanted to hear him say her name. He didn't.

"Raisa Lovell," she said, not knowing why she felt the need to say it.

"I am Jackson," he stated.

"Jackson? Just Jackson? No surname?"

"Burke."

She looked at his chest. He still held her by her arms as if supporting her from falling. She thought about dropping her knees so he'd have to lift her into his arms and carry her to the bed.

This fantasy was getting out of control.

As if realizing he held her longer than he needed to, he let her go. He kept his hands lifted as he pulled them back, testing to see if she could stay upright on her own.

"You're welcome to try the decontaminator," he motioned to a smaller door in the wall where the unit would be. "But I can't promise it will work properly."

"What about a food simulator? If you have one of those, I can use it to make myself a liquid bath. Then all I'll need is a piece of material to wipe with." Raisa had been in some primitive situations in her quest to find recipes, and it wouldn't be the first time she'd bathed out of a bowl. She had the Pha'n flower water recipe memorized. Technically, it was a watery soup, but it was fragrant and better than smelling like dirt and sweat.

"Of course, you must be hungry as well." He went toward the door that remained open. "Do you feel like you can walk?"

"The concern is appreciated, but I assure you, I'll be fine in a few days." She gingerly moved to follow him, taking smaller steps. Pride wouldn't let her turn back around and fall into the bed.

7

Jackson didn't know what to make of the woman, Raisa. It was clear she was in pain, as she limped down the metal corridor. The artificial lights flickered on the walls, some going out for several seconds before flashing back on. The ship was in bad shape.

Raisa placed her hand on the wall and closed her eyes. She took several deep breaths.

"Are you well? Do you need me to take you back?" Jackson moved as if to lift her into his arms but held back. Touching the woman had done something to his senses last time, something he didn't want to explore. He wasn't such a cad as to rescue a woman and then expect romance in return. She owed him nothing. "I should take you back to bed. You need rest."

"Your ship isn't doing so well," she said, rubbing her hand on the wall. "The nerves are weak."

"Nerves?" he questioned.

Raisa opened her eyes and looked at him. "Sorry, I meant wires. I tend to think of mechanics as living objects. The engine is the heart, the power lines the nerves, liquid tubes are like the veins."

"Computer system would be the brain," he deduced.

Raisa smiled and nodded. "Yeah, exactly. VR the imagination. And…" She let her words trail off with a soft laugh. "I sound delusional."

"No more so than our pilot. He keeps calling the ship his girl and stroking it every time we're docked." Though, comparing her to Rick might not exactly be a compliment.

Raisa pressed her cheek to the metal wall. "What's her name?"

"*Bound Virgin*," Jackson stated.

Raisa pulled away and arched a brow as she eyed him.

"I didn't name it," he defended. "It came with the ship."

"No one ever thought about changing it?" Raisa resumed her slow walk down the hall. "You know they have forms you can fill out for that."

"We have better things to spend our money on than new registration papers." Jackson didn't bother to state the other reasons. It's not like they told everyone they were pirates sailing the high skies, and a review from the ship registration office would have them poking around into ship logs, which were as fake as a pleasure droid's boobs—to paraphrase Rick.

"We?" Raisa glanced around. "How many are on board?"

As if to answer her, the sound of laughter came from the dining cabin. Jackson led her toward the others.

"The married guys are ruining it for everyone," Rick's voice drifted out. "We can't do anything fun. Viktor, back me up here. You know I just installed that extra-large viewing screen in my quarters. I haven't had a chance to use it."

"Rick, watching your transmission waves is not a vital life support system," Viktor stated, sounding distracted. He and his brother Lucien were half human, half Dere, which accounted for the unusual red-green and red-brown of their eyes. Lucien kept communications running and Viktor worked as the ship's mechanic. Since the two argued all the time, Jackson was glad only one brother was in the dining hall.

"The women will be lifelike in size," Rick insisted.

"I'm not diverting the power from the corridor

lights," Viktor denied. "You'll just have to imagine your female company like the rest of us."

"It's like I don't even know you," Rick said in mock horror.

"I can live with that," Viktor answered, his teasing tone giving away the fact they were joking around. "I like breathing more than I like you."

"What are you playing with anyway?" Rick asked.

Jackson turned into the dining cabin to find the two men were alone. Viktor had Raisa's black bag on the table and had pulled out its contents, which was mainly some kind of portable mechanical device.

"Something I found in the hall," Viktor answered. He slapped at Rick's hand as the pilot tried to touch the metal device. "You wouldn't understand it."

"What are you doing?" Raisa gasped as she hurried toward the unit.

Viktor tried to shield it with is body, as if protecting what he'd found. "I'm just looking to see if there are any parts we can scavenge to fix the—"

"Ah!" Raisa inhaled sharply. "Parts?" She slapped at Viktor's hands several times. "You will not touch my molecular gastro-spectrometer!"

"Is that what this is?" Viktor sounded more

awed than scared. "I've heard about these but have never actually seen one."

"Hey, Jackson, who's the dirty star beam?" Rick asked quietly as he sidled up next to him.

"No," Jackson stated in warning.

"But—" the pilot tried again.

"No," Jackson repeated.

"Does it work?" Viktor asked Raisa.

"Yes—no. I was on Torgan trying to get a part to fix it," she said. "Normally, yes, it works great."

"Figures." Rick gave a small laugh. "Everything on this ship is broken."

"That's a shame." Viktor frowned. "Hey, maybe we can rig it with something and get it going again? I'd love to see it in action."

"I tried. I can get it to run through the first process, but when it starts with the second it becomes unstable, and then the detector can't read the final outputs. I narrowed it down to the..." Raisa and Viktor began talking in some kind of hybrid scientist-mechanic's language. The words were understandable on their own, but strung together they made very little sense.

"I wouldn't mind getting a little dirty myself," Rick whispered, nudging Jackson with his elbow. "If you know what I'm sayin'."

"No," Jackson stated flatly. He found it best not to encourage Rick down his mischievous paths.

"Fourier transform ion cyclotron resonance…" Raisa explained to Viktor, her voice enthusiastic, as if she talked about the most fascinating thing in all the galaxies.

"Ah, that's too bad," Rick said. Jackson arched a brow in question.

"…single mass analyzer…"

"Can't be easy to see Viktor sweep in and steal your girl," continued Rick. "If I were you, I'd be embarrassed."

Jackson tensed. The two did seem to be getting along very well.

"…fragmenting molecules…"

"Maybe we should give them some privacy." Rick tapped Jackson's arm. "It's kind of like watching a first date, isn't it? They're really cute together, don't you think?"

Jackson inhaled sharply.

"…used for protein identification—"

"I thought you wanted to wash up," Jackson interrupted.

Rick snickered behind his hand, and Jackson realized the man had been goading him into a reaction. Blasted stars, it had worked too. Rick's words had wormed their way into his head.

"Oh, I, ah…" Raisa looked down at her clothes and then at Viktor. "He's right, I'm a mess."

"No more so than the rest of us." Viktor

frowned at Jackson when Raisa moved to go to the food simulator. He mouthed, "What are you doing?"

Jackson didn't have an answer.

"How old is this thing?" Raisa asked, touching their food simulator, trying to move it so she could look behind it. The unit had been bolted down. "I haven't seen this model in a long time."

"We might be in need of a few upgrades," Jackson muttered.

"Don't you have some VR monsters to fight?" Rick asked Jackson, as if dismissing him from the room.

"Can't," Viktor inserted. "VR systems are down. They take too much power."

"That explains so much," Rick chuckled. It was no secret that Jackson spent an unusual amount of time in virtual reality training. He used to exercise with Dev, but since his friend had married, he'd been fighting solo. Though, could he call it sparring if he programmed more alien foes than was physically possible to defend himself against? Sometimes he didn't even put up a fight, and he let the computer-generated warriors beat on him. The ship medic always healed him afterward, so it's not like anyone knew how bad it could be.

She ignored the two men and turned to Jackson apologetically. "I didn't mean that the way it sounded. I meant to say, this is one of the best models put out. They're heavy, but they work much longer than their lightweight counterparts. My advice would be to keep it as long as you can."

Viktor instantly moved forward, slipping his hand on top of the unit. "Are you a food simulator connoisseur?"

"Something like that," Raisa said. "I'm an Intergalactic Culinary Specialist."

"You cook?" Rick asked with interest. "Because I have to tell you, simulated food lives up to its name. It pretends to be edible."

Raisa gave a tight smile. "I'm the one who deconstructs foods and creates the parameters that make food simulation possible."

Rick arched a brow.

"I make the recipes," Raisa simplified, her tone a little flat.

"Is that so?" Rick tried to lean in front of Viktor to block the man from the exchange. "So tell me, why can't these things," he banged the top of the unit, "make a decent piece of chocolate?"

Viktor pushed Rick out of his way to rejoin the conversation.

"I heard it was because the Lithorian monks have a monopoly on chocolate making, and they threatened the simulator people," Viktor said. "It's because it's the food of the gods and they use it to lure people to their way of life."

"I've not heard of monks outright threatening anyone, but they *have* been putting political pressure on the company not to use Lithorian chocolate in their experiments. It still happens because it's the best chocolate in the universes. But no one can get it right. It's not from lack of trying. It's the one recipe none of us can figure out how to program. Every specialist I know is trying to conquer that beast. One of my colleagues came close, but it was not well received at a chocolate-tasting festival, and it had some adverse effects on a few alien species. Since then, Simulator Corp has been hesitant to release another version. It'll be a huge payday for whoever figures it out."

"Huge payday? How's this work again?" Rick placed his hand on the unit.

Jackson didn't move as he watched the two men make fools of themselves. He had no claim on the woman and she could talk to whoever she chose. That didn't mean he enjoyed Rick and Viktor fighting for her attention.

"She is injured," Jackson stated. "You should let her rest."

Raisa looked annoyed by his statement. "Yeah, apparently I'm as delicate as I am dirty." She turned to the food simulator.

Rick grinned, as if he couldn't contain himself. He started to respond but Viktor slapped his hand over the man's mouth and shook his head in denial.

Raisa didn't appear to notice as she pushed several buttons on the food simulator. She waited a few moments before pulling out a large bowl of steaming liquid. The smell of flowers filled the room. She eyed Jackson. "I'll need a cloth to wash with…and privacy."

"You can use my quarters," Rick offered. "I don't mind."

"I was thinking more the room I woke up in," she said, her eyes widening slightly as if to convey some kind of secret message to Jackson, only to add, "if it's not a problem."

"It's fine." Jackson lifted his hand to the side and gestured for her to walk before him from the room. She did, and he hovered his hand behind her back as if to protect her even as he needlessly guided her.

"Let me know if you need me to help wash your back." Rick grinned more at Jackson than Raisa. He knew he was getting under Jackson's skin.

Raisa chuckled, and he heard her mutter, "That man is a handful of trouble."

"You have no idea," Jackson answered. Lights blinked in the corridor, a constant reminder of the tin can of a broken ship they were currently flying in. The sooner they were out of Torgan airspace the better. If some unsavory characters—or the Federation Military—decided to attack, they wouldn't have the power to evade capture or defend themselves. It wasn't an ideal situation for space pirates to be in.

"It's obvious you don't like him," Raisa said. "Did something happen between the two of you? Or is it just a personality clash?"

"Who said I didn't like him?" Jackson stopped walking. The soft lights illuminated her face in small bursts, drawing his eyes to her mouth. It had been a long while since he'd been with a woman. All the females on the ship were spoken for. The places they'd landed as of late provided little opportunity. On Qurilixen, the population of shifters was predominately male, so no luck there. On Torgan, they were all thieves and outlaws, again no luck. On the last three fueling docks, the only woman he was physically compatible with had been a lykan, and she had more hair than grugs during their winter season. He and Dev had fought grugs in the VR, and Jackson had no desire to be reminded of the howling, slashing beasts while in someone's bed.

"Jackson?"

He realized he'd not heard what she had said. "I was thinking of battle and not listening. I apologize."

"Uh, okay." She gave him a quizzical look. "That's surprisingly honest of you."

"Who said I didn't like Rick?" he asked, prompting her to resume where he'd drifted off. He really needed to stop thinking about sex when talking to her. He had more self-control, and self-respect, than that.

"It was rather obvious by the way you looked at him. If I had to guess, you want to throw him off the ship," she said. "He annoys you, at the very least."

That is because the charming spacehole was flirting with you, he thought.

"Rick is family," Jackson stated so there could be no mistaking what his loyalties were. "He is like my brother, and I love him like a brother. I would give my life to protect any member of this crew."

Raisa hugged her bowl closer to her stomach and took a step back. "I apologize. I spoke out of turn."

Jackson didn't know why everything that came out of his mouth toward her sounded gruff. He wanted to say nice things, be charming and friendly. He wanted to tell her how pretty she looked, even with the dirt on her face. Or how he liked the way her animated voice lifted and dropped with enthusiasm when she spoke of scientific stuff. Or how light she was to carry in his arms. How he was sorry he'd brought her onto a broken ship. How he wanted to kiss her. How he wanted to brush the hair from her cheek. How he wanted…her.

He wanted her.

"Your dirty face…" He hesitated. That wasn't coming out right. What was it Rick would say to women he liked? That man somehow seemed to have luck with the ladies.

"Saddle up, sweet cheeks, big Rick is ready to take you for a torpedo ride."

Okay, maybe charming wasn't the right word to use to describe Rick.

"Without washing, you…" Again, he hesitated. Blasted space balls. What in the fiery depths of Bravon was wrong with him?

"Come to Rickie, baby cakes, I got everything you need right here."

"Come to…" No. He could not say that to her. How the hell did any of those lines work?

"I've heard about people having a condition where they're extremely bothered by, or even fearful of, dirt and germs, to the point they scrub themselves raw and can't think rationally," she said. "Until you, I never met anyone who had it though."

Jackson grimaced. "I'm a trained soldier. I'm not afraid of dirt."

He wanted to say he wasn't afraid of anything, but that wasn't true. He was afraid of losing his crewmates. They were the only family he had.

"Okay, if you say so." Her voice lifted in a way that said she didn't believe him but wasn't about to argue the point.

"You're pretty, just like that," he said.

"Are you...?" She arched a brow. "You know what, never mind. It's not important. How about you show me where I can clean up?"

Jackson nodded, deciding it was best if he didn't say anything else.

8

"*You're pretty…*"

Raisa shook her head as she remembered his words. Not so much what he said but the difficulty the words seemed to bring him. Poor Jackson. Being a soldier had clearly taken its toll on him.

Raisa had seen such injuries before—one too many blows to the head without prompt medical treatment caused the wits to slow. It was too bad. He seemed like a nice guy. Clearly, he was the ship muscle, evident by his incredible build. And he was handsome. Well, that really didn't have anything to do with anything. She supposed a person didn't need wits to fight, not really, not when he had brute strength on his side.

She did her best to wash with a cloth and bowl without getting too much water on the decontaminator floor. Even so, it felt good to be clean. Bending over still hurt, but the healing bruise over her ribs was doing what it was meant to.

"I found clothes," Jackson said from the other side of the decontaminator door. She liked the sound of his deep voice. "You look to be about Violette's size."

His words were calm and confident, as they had been when they first spoke, not stuttering and strange like they'd been when walking back from the dining hall. Maybe she'd misjudged, and her first impression was correct. He wasn't dimwitted, only an extreme germaphobe.

"Who else is on this ship?" she asked, keeping the conversation going.

"Viktor's brother Lucien is our communications man."

"They're Dere, aren't they? It looks like they have yet to go through their chrysalis." The opaque complexion and red tinted eyes gave it away.

"I don't believe they will. They're half human." Jackson's voice seemed to come from the direction of the bed. "Lochlann is our captain. His wife, Alexis, is our intelligence officer. These are their quarters. Dev and his wife Violette are security officers. She sometimes helps to pilot the ship. That's everyone. We're a small crew."

"And you?"

"I am also a security officer."

"Why so much security? Are you transporting something important?" She wondered what kind of cargo they could be carrying to warrant so much protection.

"How did you begin formulating recipes?" Jackson avoided answering.

Raisa tried to open the door wide enough to peek through, but it didn't stop as she pressed the button. It opened completely, revealing her naked body to Jackson.

The wet cloth floated in the bowl and wouldn't be big enough to cover much anyway. He sat on the corner of the bed, facing her. She gasped, looking for a way to cover up. Her foot bumped the bowl of dirty water, sloshing a little onto the decontaminator floor. She tried to cover her breasts with her hands, not that she was necessarily modest, but there was something powerful happening between them that caused her to tremble.

Cooler air hit her damp skin, and she shivered. Jackson didn't turn away as he stared at her. His breathing audibly deepened. His lips parted, and his eyes narrowed as they swept over her form.

She opened her mouth to speak but he stood,

cutting off her words before they could even make it past her throat. His eyes lifted and met hers. He came toward her like a heat-seeking missile toward a star.

"I…" He stopped before her. She shivered anew.

Jackson lifted his hand to her face, as if testing her reaction to his touch. The warmth of his fingers was a stark contrast to the chill. Her breathing deepened. She lifted a hand away from her chest and placed it on his. His fingers moved down her cheek to her neck, where his palm flattened against her shoulder. The movement was torturous and slow. She knew she should stop and consider her situation, but logic had no place in how she was feeling. Every nerve seemed to spark beneath her skin, enticing her toward him like a magnet to metal.

Missiles to stars? Magnets to metal? When did she begin thinking like a bad poet?

Once she touched Jackson, she couldn't pull away. Her head tilted back and he took the invitation to skim his hand down her chest to cup a breast. She inhaled softly as his palm hit the aching tip. With each breath, her nipple rubbed his calloused hand, sending pleasure over her. His other hand touched her stomach, lightly running over where the healing bruise had formed. It created a shell of sorts around her nerves, and she couldn't feel that touch as deeply. Her lips remained parted and she waited for him to kiss her. She wanted the hand on her stomach to move lower, to where her thighs guarded her sex.

"I've had my shots. I can't get pregnant," was all she could think to say when he didn't move his body closer.

He seemed to be struggling with an inner turmoil. Finally, he moaned, "Me, too," followed by a desperate sound as he captured his mouth with hers.

His kiss was both passionate and gentle. Her back hit the doorframe of the decontaminator. The sharp edge pressed into her skin, but she didn't want his lips to stop.

Her hands were trapped between her breasts and his chest. His hands slid down her damp sides to her hips, only to pull her forward against his arousal. The full length of him was unmistakably hard.

Without seeming to use much effort, he cupped her ass and lifted her off the ground to better angle her hips to his. This drew her center up along his shaft. The hot feel of his erection through his clothes rubbed against her in a way that was all too pleasurable. She wriggled her arms free and wrapped them around his neck to help support her weight. His hips rocked forward, as if he could already feel himself inside her. She reached between them, cupping his arousal.

"Jackson, the guys could use your— *Oh, sacre*— sorry, sorry, I didn't see anything!" a woman exclaimed in obvious shock. A slap sounded, followed by another. "What's wrong with the door, it won't let me out." The slapping became more frantic. "Why won't it let me out?"

Raisa braced herself, too shocked to move.

"Computer, open door," the woman ordered. The computer didn't answer.

Jackson released Raisa and firmly urged her into the decontaminator before standing in front of the door to block her nudity.

"Violette, the door is not going to work until the power cycles back around," Jackson said.

"So," Violette drawled. "How's it going? Anything new with you, Jackson?"

Jackson didn't answer.

Raisa stared at Jackson's back. She inhaled deeply and held her breath in an attempt to slow her breathing. If this Violette woman hadn't interrupted them, she would not have stopped what was happening. Even now, she could feel the sting of his kisses and the pleasure of his hands. Her body ached to continue, so much so that she didn't even feel the pain in her ribs.

"Who's your friend?" Violette asked, as if Jackson's silence didn't bother her.

"Raisa," she answered loudly. Raisa moved her hand around Jackson and blindly waved. "Nice to meet you."

Violette laughed, but Raisa felt the woman touch her finger. "And you as well."

"Thank you for letting me borrow clothes," Raisa said, remembering what Jackson had said earlier.

"How about I turn around so you have a chance to wear them?" Violette offered.

Jackson stepped aside and crossed to the bed. Raisa slowly followed him. She glanced at Violette. The taller woman stood with her back to them. Her brown hair curled to her shoulders. She wore tight brown pants with a red top that had a triangle pattern cut out over her back. It left her skin around her waist bare. Green markings encircled her waist, as if tattooed into her flesh.

Jackson handed her a stack of clothes, and she realized she was staring at the woman while standing naked. The black pants fit all right but were a little long at the ankles. The black shirt was adjustable by white cross-laces along the arms and sides.

As she pulled the strings near her waist to tighten them, she said, "Done."

Violette turned. Mischievous green eyes met hers. "Looks good on you. Go ahead and keep them."

"Thank you." Raisa glanced down at herself and then at Jackson, who still didn't speak.

"Doesn't she look good, Jackson?" Violette prompted.

"Yes." The answer was short and matter-of-fact.

"Isn't he just a charmer?" Violette laughed, only to sarcastically add, "A man of many words."

Jackson made a soft, unamused sound.

"Take it easy," Violette told Jackson. "I'm only teasing." Then to Raisa, she said, "Must be a security officer thing. My husband can be a man of few words as well."

"What did you need help with?" Jackson asked.

"What? Oh, yeah." Violette nodded. "The guys need you to help move a metal grate, so they can get behind the wall. Have you seen the back corridor yet? It's beginning to look like a warzone. I'm beginning to question if they actually know what they're doing, or if Viktor and Alexis just guess and hope for the best."

Jackson went to the door and tried the hand scanner. It didn't work.

"They will send someone when I don't return. I told them I'd be right back." Violette moved toward the cage in the middle of the room and wrapped her hand around a metal bar. "This ship is just…" She didn't finish the thought but shook her head in what looked to be disapproval.

Raisa watched her walk around to the other side of the cage. She found herself following her. A small living area was set up around the corner. She hadn't looked at it before. Two black couches with red throw pillows stretched nearly all the way across the alcove. A viewing screen had been mounted in front. Violette sat on one of the low couch backs, before letting herself fall onto the cushions. Her feet hung over the back, kicking lazily.

"You never think about how much we rely on electricity until you don't have it," Raisa said by way of conversation.

"Especially out here in the deep black," Violette agreed. "No transmission waves to watch. No VR. One can only listen to Jackson and Dev running around the corridors exercising for so long."

"We will have to watch each other for signs of isolation sickness." Jackson crossed his arms over his chest. It was becoming a familiar stance. "With no distractions, this could be a long ride."

"I have a natural knack for fixing mechanical things," Raisa offered.

Violette leaned up, letting her feet drop to the couch so she could study Raisa.

"What do you mean?" Jackson asked.

"It's always come easy to me. I just understand mechanical things—engines, personal droids, cleaning droids, generators, appliances, and even electrical systems." Raisa moved to sit on the couch but didn't fall onto the cushions like Violette, instead choosing to walk around before taking a seat.

"Are you..." Violette tilted her head as she studied her. "Angelion?"

"Half," Raisa answered. "How did you know that? No one ever guesses."

"Gil, the mechanic on a ship I used to captain, was Angelion," Violette said. "He could tighten bolts without touching them, sense when something wasn't right behind a wall, and was one of the grumpiest men I'd ever worked with—not that you're grumpy. He was one of the best mechanics I've ever seen."

Raisa gave a small nod.

"My husband is half Bevlon. That's not going to be a problem for you, is it?" Violette asked. Bevlons and Angelions were ancient enemies.

"Not at all. I barely knew my father," Raisa said. "I have no interest in ancient battles."

"Glad to hear it." Violette nodded. "Jackson, you should let her take a look at the ship. Trust me. Alexis and Viktor need all the help they can get."

Raisa glanced up at Jackson. "I would like to help. It's the least I can do."

He gave her a small smile and nodded once. "As soon as you feel up to it."

"Can you fix the door?" Violette asked.

"Not if it doesn't have a power supply." Raisa couldn't create electricity, only direct where it flowed.

"Hey, did you space cadets lock yourselves in?" Rick called from the other room.

"Rick!" Violette hopped up from the couch. "Don't let the door shut. It's broken."

"I have to do everything around here," Rick teased. "Don't worry, ladies, Rick is here to rescue you."

Jackson waited for Raisa to follow Violette before walking behind her. Rick stood in the doorway, his hand pressed to the top of the frame as if he alone kept the door from sliding shut.

"Oh, I guess I'll save you too, big guy," Rick joked.

Raisa found the man both charming and cocky. He had an easy nature that was welcoming, if not slightly inappropriate, which was great in a social situation. But as a spaceship pilot? She wasn't sure this guy was serious enough to handle a big piece of equipment.

He winked at her. "What do you know, there was a pretty lady underneath all that grime."

Jackson stood a little bit closer to her. The heat

radiating off him only reminded her of what they'd been interrupted doing. "Raisa is going to assist us in repairs."

"Good deal." Rick stepped out into the corridor and pet the metal wall. The door remained open. "My sweet lady needs all the help she can get."

9

Raisa ignored the pain in her side as she pressed between the metal wall and the jumbled mess of wires that seemed to lead nowhere. None of it made logical sense. Some of them looped around, only to head back in the direction from which they came. Others were spliced together in ways she wouldn't consider safe. Honestly, it was a wonder the ship had flown as long as it had.

"Well?" Viktor's voice called from the opening in the wall. She shone her handheld light toward him but couldn't make out his face. The hand strap was broken, so she had to grip the rectangular device with her fingers. "See anything?"

Raisa placed her hands on the wires, trying to feel where the currents flowed. Some were completely dead. She found one that felt hot to the touch and appeared to be pulling more current than it should. "Maybe. I'm going to follow—"

"No, that's far enough. Come out," Jackson called. "It's not safe. We're having a hard time seeing you."

She gave a small laugh at his order, even as she followed the wire away from the wall opening. "Come in here and make me."

"What is it with the female crew we take on always crawling into tight spaces?" Viktor asked, his voice softer than before. "Mei in the ceiling. Alexis in the air vents. Raisa in the walls. Violette, you have any urges to crawl under the floor grates?"

"Whose Mei?" Raisa called, feeling comforted by the sound of voices. The light she carried didn't reveal much but dust and wires.

"The wife of Jackson and Lochlann's original captain," Viktor answered. "They live on Qurilixen."

"Never heard of it," Raisa said.

"They're a bunch of shifter—*hey, watch it,*" Viktor made a small sound of irritation.

"As the ship security officer, I command—" Jackson tried to order.

She laughed louder, cutting him off. "Take it easy. I know what I'm doing."

Raisa hoped she was right. She didn't feel any

immediate danger, but the system was unstable. She inched along the inside of the wall, trying not to scrape her back on the rows of bolts holding the wall panels in place. As she moved, she tapped her fingers to the hot wire to follow where it led.

"Raisa?" she heard Jackson yell.

"I'm fine," she reassured him. His concern was both annoying and sweet—maybe more annoying than sweet. She was a grown woman who had made her way around the high skies and numerous planets just fine. Sure, Torgan wasn't a prime example of that, but hey, here she was—alive.

Her light shone over a bracket that had a screw loose. She automatically lifted her hand, willing the screw to tighten. It moved without her having to touch it.

The wires continued to thread in various directions, some up to the ceiling or into the floor. What in the galaxies was going on in this ship? She followed the hot wire, ducking under cold pipes as she was led deeper into the ship, away from the wall. Bundles of tubes were strung together, possibly for the in-room medics. She came to an area that had a little more space to maneuver in, probably to allow for repairs. She followed the wire until it disappeared into a wall.

Raisa felt along a bolted seam. Most of them had been welded shut, but for a small access panel near the floor. She flattened her hand and hovered it over the bolts, causing them to slowly unscrew, one by one. Without this gift, she wouldn't have been able to open the panel. The bolts clanked on the other side of the barrier. When she'd finished, she tried to push the panel. It wouldn't move. She searched for something to wedge into the sides to pry it out, and in the end had to use her short nails. With considerable effort, she managed to loosen it enough that she could will it out of the wall. She hovered her hands over it and pulled at the metal. It fell in her lap.

Raisa shone her light into the dark hole, expecting to see more access corridors and wires. Nothing else should be this deep in the ship's belly.

As her light hit a smooth white floor, she wasn't so sure. She glanced at the panel she'd pulled. It was sprayed with a thick white lacquer and had a foreign word painted on it. She assumed to mark it as an access panel.

She knelt close to the floor and flashed her light, trying to see inside. Metal posts held a platform, so she couldn't look up. Clutching her light, she cautiously crawled forward. Whatever this dark room was it hummed with power.

She thought she heard an echo of her name but ignored the shout. Fear crept over her, knotting her stomach with anticipation and dread. Whatever this room was, it didn't feel like it belonged in this ship.

The floor was cool to the touch as she made her way inside. She bumped her knee on the access hatch and the light dropped to the floor. At the sound of the crash, lights illuminated the room.

Raisa pressed her lips tightly together to keep from gasping and held very still. When nothing moved, she slowly made her way from under a table and stood.

The small room had been painted white with the same plastic lacquer of the panel door. The concave molding between the floor and walls erased any sense of an edge. Aside from the gray metal table, the floor space was empty. Two walls were filled with small, transparent drawers. They looked to be full of vials. A holographic screen descended from the ceiling, but the menu was unreadable. She felt more than heard an air vent pulling air from the room and guessed that was why it lacked the dust that filled the corridors.

As she walked, the floor vibrated and opened. A padded medical chair rose into the center of the room. The gears made no sound except for a light *thunk-thunk* when it fitted and latched into place. Clearly made for humanoids, the table had leg and arm extensions and straps.

Raisa held very still, unsure what to make of the

room, only to feel a strong sense that she should not have found it. Seeing a seam that had to be the way out, she reached into the crawlspace and pulled the panel back into place, using small grooves on the white side to hold it. It suctioned and sealed the moment it touched it against the wall. The air vent stopped and silence filled the room.

Raisa walked cautiously around the chair. She lifted her hand to touch a glass drawer holding the vials. At the contact, a small screen lit up like an inventory of that container.

"*Rinabac, Grarf, Tolofat, Lithemadix*." She read the alien words. Were these medications? Some of the markings on the vials looked vaguely familiar, but she wasn't a doctor.

"Computer?" she asked.

A low tone sounded, as if to signify the mainframe did not recognize her.

Where in all the Bravon fire balls was she? Who were these people? Why did they have a secret operating room in the middle of their ship?

The wall opened, and a small orb appeared. It drifted forward. Raisa held up her hand defensively to block lights as the unit scanned her. A hard zap hit the tip of her finger, causing it to bleed as if she'd pricked it on a needle. She stuck the finger in her mouth as the orb retracted the way it came.

"Message received," she mumbled, "the grumpy computer doesn't want to talk."

When nothing else happened, she turned back to the inventory screen.

Raisa lightly pressed her finger to the word *Grarf* to see if the drawer would open. It was stupid. She realized that the moment she touched it. She glanced back to the wall to make sure the orb didn't return.

The vials within the drawer moved and she saw a needle come down and pull liquid out of the vial. She couldn't see where it went, but she closed her eyes to sense if there were any changes in the electrics or mechanics of the unit. Following a tingling sensation with her Angelion senses, she heard a small hissing noise, and then a series of clicks.

"What have you done now, Raisa?" she whispered to herself. She looked up to make sure nothing was going to come from the ceiling and inject her like in the captain's quarters. She had no idea what these vials were—medicines, biological weapons, poisons—or what species they were intended for.

When the *Grarf* didn't appear to do anything, she inched her way toward the door. It was smooth with no handle or hand scanner. As she touched the surface, the door opened to let her pass into a dark hall.

Realizing she still clutched the light, she shone it into the short passageway before stepping in. The door closed behind her, leaving her in the dark a few seconds before another flat holographic image appeared about an inch away from the far wall. This time it was a floating, floor-length viewing screen of one of the ship's main corridors. A small button flashed in the corner, only to freeze when Lucien ran past. Once he was gone, the button flashed again.

As Raisa walked toward the hologram, she detected movement on her left. She jolted in alarm, turning to find a humanoid behind a transparent panel.

She pulled back in fright and the light slipped from her fingers. She scrambled to pick it up.

Her hands shaking, Raisa shone her light upward to find a stasis chamber. The soft glow of the holographic image gave little illumination. In the chamber, the humanoid's blue-tinted skin almost seemed to reflect the blue bedding, until Raisa realized it wasn't bedding but a shimmering gown covering the woman from neck to calves.

"Hey, Blue," Raisa whispered, giving her the only name she could think of in her nervous state. "What are you doing in here?"

She waited in apprehension as she shone the light on Blue's face to watch for signs of life. Blue didn't move. Her dark hair was brushed back behind her. Someone had taken great care in laying her out for hypersleep. Raisa drew the light down over the woman's shoulder and arm. Peeks of Blue's dark hair could be seen along her waist. Her hands rested at her sides, the nails long. Her feet were bare, with five elongated toes on each.

The movement Raisa had seen was an injector retracting from the woman's arm.

Oops. Did I do that?

Raisa shone the light on the woman's face, watching to see if anything changed after the shot. There were no signs of life. Blue looked frozen in time. The *Grarf*, if that was what was injected, didn't appear to have an effect.

Raisa turned to look at the opposite wall. Instead of a stasis chamber, there was a tank filled with a dark substance. She crept closer, pressing the light to the transparent barrier to try to see what was inside. As she slid it along the tank, she found a skeletal frame floating in the dark liquid.

Her breath caught and held. The creature was not exactly humanoid, in the sense it had eight bony protrusions coming from the waist like the legs of a spider, but the torso and arms of a man.

Raisa hurried toward the image of the ship's

corridor. Jackson ran past the screen as she tried to press the frozen button. It didn't move. She pressed it again and again, trying to get out. Only when Jackson was out of sight did a door swing toward her on electric hinges, letting her walk through the corridor's wall. As she stepped out, she pressed her back to the far wall and watched as the door close.

She slid down the wall and sat on the floor.

"Do you hear anything?" Jackson yelled.

"Raisa," one of the men yelled from the direction Lucien had gone.

"Raisa," came another voice from the opposite way.

They were searching inside the walls for her.

She tried to answer, but her voice caught and she had to swallow. Her hands trembled and, for a moment, as she stared at the very normal-looking wall, she wondered if she'd hallucinated the secret medical chamber.

"Start removing every fifth panel," Jackson ordered. "Hurry. Let's find her. She's been out of contact too long." He came around the corner mumbling, "I knew it was a bad idea to let her go in there. Hardheaded woman—" The last word was cut off as he stumbled to a stop. "Raisa?"

"I…" She lifted a finger to point at the wall.

"I found her," Jackson yelled as he rushed toward her.

"I found…" She tried again. Her heart beat incredibly fast, and she felt lightheaded as if the adrenaline levels in her body suddenly dropped.

"Raisa?" Jackson knelt beside her. His concerned eyes held her gaze. "Why didn't you answer me when I called?"

"Where was she?" Viktor asked. He jogged down the corridor, followed by Lochlann and Alexis. She'd only met Lochlann in passing, but he seemed a decent fellow. Definitely not one to captain a crew with strange tank creatures and woman in stasis next to a secret laboratory. Lucien, Violette, and Dev came from the other direction.

"Where did you come from?" Lucien asked. "We were on both ends of this corridor. How did you slip past us?"

She took a deep breath and gestured at the wall. It occurred to her that the room she'd been in was soundproofed. She hadn't heard their calls for her after she'd sealed herself in. "I might have found your problem."

"Is there a loose connection behind that panel?" Alexis asked, placing her hand on the wall. Her eyes took on a faraway look, as if she wasn't seeing her hand but something in her mind. "The schematics I downloaded don't have anything of importance in this location, some communications wires and possibly suction delivery tubes, which was an optional installation when these ships were purchased new, though I haven't seen evidence of any."

Raisa tried to stand, uncomfortable with the way they crowded around her and looked down as she sat on the floor. Jackson took her arm and helped guide her up the wall. She continued to lean against it, not because she needed the support, but because the corridor was full. As far as she knew, the only person on the ship that was missing was Rick, who was probably piloting the craft.

Oh, and the blue lady behind the wall.

She cleared her throat. "The electrical malfunction was most likely caused by a significant power drain on your system, which took priority over all else. Rick mentioned he had a new viewing screen installed in his quarters. If you all installed new technology, and simply spliced into existing connections, it was only a matter of time before it overloaded the grid."

"I knew Rick was to blame," Viktor said.

"One viewing screen wouldn't have done it. I'm guessing it was a bunch of little things over the years. There is a lot of bizarre wiring choices in this ship. Wires loop for no discernable reason. Things are spliced and connected. I even saw a length of wire that had been cut and repaired in two spots rather than running a whole new line."

Everyone turned to look at Viktor.

Viktor lifted his hands. "Hey, I've been telling you all for years I'm just patching things together, and that we needed to put more money into real repairs. No one cared as long as I could keep us limping along."

Raisa felt a little sorry for him, so she added, "I'm guessing a lot of these repairs were done before you came into possession of the ship. Unless you've been flying it for thirty or forty years?"

"Ha! See, not my fault." Viktor smiled as if vindicated. "Still Rick's doing."

Raisa watched them all carefully as she spoke. Not one of them gave any indication they were worried by what was behind the wall. It was possible they didn't know.

"How did you get this ship?" she asked.

"Our former captain, Samantha, won it in a high-stakes card game," said Lucien.

"Gambling?" Raisa repeated in surprise. "So you didn't have it inspected before you flew?"

"We looked at it," Viktor said.

"It's flown just fine," Lucien added.

"We didn't have a sale inspection," Dev clarified. The man was unnerving as he towered over them. It wasn't his red skin or dark eyes, but the stern way he stared at her, like she was a child in trouble. Or maybe it was the reminder that his

Bevlon side and her Angelion side were supposed to hate each other. Raisa had no reason to hate him.

"Why do you ask?" Jackson studied her. "What does this have to do with the power drain on the ship?"

Raisa wasn't sure how to start, so she stepped toward the wall that had opened into the secret room and ran a hand over the metal. Aside from the normal seams, it looked like any other section of hall. "I don't know how to open it."

"Do you want me to get the tools?" Viktor offered, already rushing away to do just that.

"What are you looking for?" Jackson asked, placing his hand on the smooth surface.

"There's this room," she tried to explain. "On the other side of this wall."

"You sense the mechanics behind the wall?" asked Violette.

"No. Yes, but no," Raisa said, aware that all eyes were on her. "The wall opens. I walked out of it. There is this corridor that leads to a white room, and…"

As she spoke she watched their expressions move from listening to doubtful to concerned.

Jackson placed a hand on her shoulder. "It's all right, Raisa. We should never have let you go inside the walls to check. It's not safe in there. Maybe the pain medicine I gave you is having a strange side effect, and you're seeing things. We should get you back to bed so you can heal."

"Let me try this from the other direction. I was in the wall looking at your wiring system—which is messier than lykan fur, for the record—and I found a hot wire that was drawing more power than is normal for a ship, especially considering the current power fluctuations. I followed the wire—"

"Were you electrocuted?" Lucien guessed.

"No. I followed it to an access panel. I pulled it out and crawled into a secret room on this ship. It was white, with an alien language I couldn't understand, and there were these vials, and a surgical medical chair shaped for humanoids, with straps. And I pushed a vial button that ended up injecting—"

"You injected yourself with an alien drug?" Violette questioned.

"No, I injected…" She frowned. They were having a hard time believing her. She couldn't blame them. This was their ship and she was new to them. They didn't know if she had a history of insanity. Claiming there was a dead alien and a woman in some kind of a hypersleep chamber wouldn't help her case.

"Yes?" Jackson prompted. His gaze was worried, but he didn't look at her like the others. He was trying to believe her.

"There was an orb and it zapped my finger." Her fingertip had a spot of drying blood on it and she held it up as proof.

"It's all right, Raisa." Jackson moved to place his arm around her shoulders. "We'll keep an eye on the wall so you don't need to worry. You concentrate on rest. You've been through a lot."

"No!" Raisa slipped out from his hold and slapped her hand against the wall. This time she made contact with her bleeding finger. "It was right *here.*"

As the tiny drop of her blood touched the metal, the wall absorbed the red smear.

"What just happened?" Dev asked, trying to protectively force his wife behind his back. Violette grimaced in annoyance and pushed her way back around to watch.

The wall made a noise. Jackson placed a hand on her shoulder and tried to urge her away.

"What's it doing?" Alexis asked.

The hidden door opened, swinging inward to reveal the corridor.

"I told you!" Raisa exclaimed. "There's a secret room."

"Holy black hole." Viktor dropped the tools he carried. "What did you guys do?"

Raisa tried to step inside. Both Dev and Jackson grabbed her arms to hold her back.

"I want to go," Alexis said, sounding excited.

"I want to see, too," Violette added.

"I'm good. You have fun," said Lucien.

"As security officers, only Jackson and I will go in," Dev decided.

"I've already been in. Besides, you need me to open doors." Raisa lifted her finger. She had no idea if that were true or not. "It has my blood profile on file now."

Dev sighed.

Jackson reluctantly nodded. "Stay between us."

Jackson stepped in first. Raisa followed him, only to stop in the doorway and reach back. "Viktor, hand me my light?"

He fumbled to pick it up from the floor but finally handed it over.

The corridor walls were now empty. "There were two…"

"Two what?" Dev started to follow her—but the door closed behind her to lock him out.

10

Raisa reached forward to stop the door from closing, but Jackson pulled her against his chest and wrapped a protective arm around her waist. He lifted his free hand and looked around, ready for anything that might come at them. The holographic image showed Dev pounding his fist against the outside wall, but sound didn't pass through the barrier.

"What is this place?" Jackson's chest rose and fell against her back. His breathing had quickened, but he didn't appear scared, and she found she wasn't as frightened with him next to her.

"I don't know. Some kind of laboratory." She shone the light on the wall. The barrier had opened up once more to reveal the woman in hypersleep. "There. She looks alive, but it's hard to tell."

Jackson placed his hand against the transparent wall before knocking a few times. She wasn't sure if he tried get the woman's attention or tested the strength of the barrier.

When nothing happened, she shone the light to the other side. "And there. This one is dead." She slid the light against the wall until the bones of the floating skeleton could be seen.

"What were you saying about a white room?" Jackson asked.

"Should we try to let Dev in first?" She motioned to where the others were studying the wall as Dev tried to swipe his blood across the door. It didn't open but did flash a warning symbol over the whole hologram.

"What language is that?" Jackson touched the holographic image of his friends.

"I have no idea," Raisa said, "and I've traveled extensively for work. I've seen a lot of writing."

"I can't believe these two have been in here the entire time we've been on this ship." Jackson looked at the blue woman, as if he could find a clue as to who she was.

"What about Dev?" Raisa lifted her hand but the button that would open the door to let them out had stopped blinking. "Blast it, I forgot. I don't think it will open unless no one is in the hall outside. It's a safety thing. I tried to escape but it wouldn't let me while you were running past."

"Great. If I know Dev, he won't leave the corridor unattended until we come back out." Jackson felt around in the dark. "How do we get to the white room?"

"This way." Raisa went to the wall opposite the image of Dev. It opened when she touched the door. She stepped into the darkness, letting her steps sound loudly. The lights activated. The chair in the middle of the room was gone and all the panels were turned off.

Jackson tried to cross the center of the room toward the vials. As the floor vibrated lightly beneath her feet, she grabbed his arm. When he glanced at her, she nodded to where the floor opened, and the surgical chair rose into place. She then pointed upward where the holographic screen would appear from the ceiling. Seconds later, it did.

"It's the same language as the door." She gestured to the screen. "I didn't touch it."

"Probably a good call until we can figure out what this place is."

"I did touch a drawer. It won't open but it pulls up an inventory list." She pressed her finger against one to show him. "But don't select anything. I think it injects the woman with it."

Jackson nodded. His expression gave none of his thoughts away as he looked around.

"I know one thing for sure. This system takes a lot of power to keep running. Do you notice the lights don't flicker in here? I think this is wired as a priority power system, with probably a reserve hold. The fact that no one knew it was here means it's on its own grid and not in the ship's mainframe. But it's drawing power from the main supply. That's why the electrical system malfunctioned. This room probably ran a command function, which caused the other overloaded grid to blow. The gas pocket igniting was an unfortunate consequence. With these doors and chair lifts, if we tore apart the walls, we might find something to rig the propulsion system until you found the right part, and the easiest way to repair the ship's electrical systems will be to shut down this room, but all the data in these systems might be lost."

"The woman in hypersleep," Jackson said. "It could kill her. We can't do that. There's a chance she is alive."

"It could wake her up," Raisa countered. Though she agreed he had a point. She didn't want to kill anyone.

"She could be dangerous, or diseased, or the nicest person to fly though the deep black," Jackson said. "We need more information."

A hissing sound started behind the wall and Jackson moved to place himself in front of Raisa. A drawer closer to the ceiling lit up. It sounded as if medicine was being taken from one of the vials.

"I will bring Alexis back and see if she can find the meaning of these words," Jackson decided. "Show me how you gave the room your blood sample so I can do the same."

"I tried to vocally activate the computer and it sent out a ball to investigate."

"Computer, take my sample so I may enter this room," Jackson commanded.

A series of beeps sounded, and then the low tone she'd heard before. The orb did not come.

"Computer?" Raisa tried.

The low tone repeated. The orb came from the wall. It did a quick scan of Raisa, only to dismiss her. Jackson lifted his chin, unafraid as it came toward him and began shining its light on him. He tilted his head one way and then the other, before walking around it. The orb turned with him, as if watching him.

"It seemed to recognize our use of the Old Star Language when you called it. The military had these. They're scanning orbs used in security facilities." He watched it carefully. "What is it waiting for?"

"Lift your hand." Raisa flinched when he lifted

his hand, only to be zapped by the orb. Jackson didn't so much as blink at the prick. The orb retracted. "That's it."

"I've seen enough. Let's get out of here."

"Dev has to leave the door," she said.

"Where is the access panel?"

"Under that table. But it's too small for you to fit through." She knelt on the floor to look at the hatch. "I can try to make my way back out and tell the others to leave the corridor. Touch the inner door to open it. There is a blinking button on the outer door. Push it when everyone is gone."

He nodded. "Be careful."

Raisa placed her hand on the panel and pushed. It didn't move. She focused her gift to make it open. It resisted. She frowned and pushed harder. "It came out before."

Jackson leaned over to watch as she slapped her hand against it. "Let me try."

She crawled out. He stood on a knee, lifted his other leg, and kicked. It didn't budge. He tried several more times.

"I think it's jammed in there," she said. "I guess this means we wait together by the door. How long can those guys stay out there watching the wall? They'll have to leave at some point."

11

Hours. The answer to her rhetorical question was hours.

Jackson stretched his legs as he sat with his back to the skeleton tank, watching Dev pace outside the door, trying to get in. The man had tried prying it open, smearing blood on it, kicking it, hitting it, burning it with a torch, and nothing had worked. Now he'd taken to glaring at it, as if he could will it open.

Every member of the crew came by at one point. Each cutting themselves and trying to use their blood as Raisa had. Alexis had gone into one of her download trances, as if trying to find a command that would vocally open the door. Again, nothing they tried worked. It was like watching a soundless transmission.

"I vote we start pushing buttons and see what happens," she said, not for the first time.

Jackson's training had taught him patience. If he had to, he could sit in a dark room for days not making a noise. As far as waiting went, this wasn't too bad. He had company, who also happened to be pretty to look at.

The handheld light was on the floor, shining up at the ceiling. It cast shadows over her face, throwing her features into stark contrast. The soft glow of the floating image in front of the door helped a little, and he saw better once his eyes had adjusted to the dark. Her dark hair was cut at an angle, falling longer by the front of her shoulders than at the nape of her neck. He was content to stare at her, liking the way she moved and laughed. She spoke with an animated quality that lit up her brown-green eyes.

"He'll have to give up eventually, right?" Raisa didn't sound so sure. She sat across from Jackson, her feet stretched out near his hips. Every once in a while, her foot would tap against him as she moved them from side to side. Each time reminded him of holding her, kissing her, and as uncomfortable as arousal made him, considering the circumstance, he didn't dare move away from her or else the contact would stop.

"You don't know Dev," Jackson said. He

couldn't blame the guy. If it was him, he'd never give up either if he had people trapped somewhere.

They'd discussed the different places they'd been, and strange beings they'd met. She spoke of the nuances of creating dishes for the simulators, and some of the weirder foods she'd tasted in the name of her job. He didn't understand all of it but liked the enthusiasm in her voice as she spoke of molecular science. He did not speak of his time in the military, beyond telling her he had been a soldier. Those were not stories he wanted her to hear.

"This is boring." Raisa yawned after a comfortable silence had fallen over them. She didn't appear scared, and for that he was grateful. "Know any games we can play?" She tilted her head to speak toward the dark tank. "Greg? No?" Then tilting her head back to talk to the woman stuck in hypersleep behind her, she asked, "What about you, Blue?"

"I get Blue, but why Greg?"

"He needed a name," Raisa answered. "And Greg was this guy I met on a fueling dock who was all hands. He kept trying to grab me so I kicked him in his man bits."

Jackson frowned. "It is not safe for a woman to travel through deep space alone. Fueling docks are dangerous and—"

"Easy, boy." Raisa lifted her hands. "If I wanted

a safety lesson I would have asked. I am quite capable of taking care of myself."

"I didn't mean to imply otherwise, but the fueling docks are—"

"Hey, so, what was that all about back at the decontaminator?" she interrupted.

If she had wanted to disarm his train of thought, she'd picked the perfect topic. He had been trying very hard not to remember the feel of her soft body along his as he'd pressed her against the decontaminator door frame. Every time he caught a whiff of the flower water she'd bathed with it stirred his body anew. He'd been able to stay focused so long as he kept thinking of all the dangers they could face in this secret chamber. If he was focused on protecting her, he wouldn't think about pressing her up against the wall.

"Are you asking me...?" Jackson frowned, not following what she meant by her question. "What are you asking me?"

"That was my indelicate way of changing the subject while bringing up what happened between us." Raisa gave a small laugh. "I'm sorry we were interrupted."

Jackson couldn't help the smile that crossed his features. He drew his knee up, draping his wrist over it. What man wouldn't be pleased to hear such a thing from a beautiful woman? "I, too, am sorry we were interrupted."

He didn't mean for his voice to drop in tone but couldn't seem to help himself. His breathing deepened as she sat forward.

"Would it be strange if I kissed you?" she asked.

He shook his head in denial, even as he said, "Maybe a little, considering the company."

She glanced at Dev. He paced back and forth as if talking to someone. "I admit, it's not the most romantic of places, but we're alone. No one can hear us. And there is definitely no chance of anyone walking in on us." She glanced up at the dark tank. "Greg, cover your eyes."

Jackson considered himself a practical man, but with the way she smiled at him, he'd have done anything she wanted. When she continued toward him, her lips parting as her eyes dipped to his mouth, he did not need to be convinced.

Her lips brushed his in a soft kiss. The firm pressure gently urged his mouth to open. He didn't move to touch her as he let her take the lead, curious as to what she would do next.

Raisa was clearly a woman who knew what she wanted. She was confident, smart, and had an adventurous spirit. Confronting the thieves on Torgan proved she was brave, if not a little reckless.

She chatted about nothing, easily carrying a conversation. Jackson knew he wasn't the most forthcoming when it came to discourse. No one ever accused him of being talkative. Raisa didn't appear to mind. She also had a way of drawing words out of him.

She pulled back, on her hands and knees in front of him. The taste of her was on his lips. Her breath tickled his cheek as she tilted to the side to whisper, "I would say I've wanted to do that from the first moment I saw you, but I was beat up on the floor fighting those whatchamacallits."

"Dokka," he supplied.

"Yeah, those galactic tear holes."

"I don't recall hearing of the whatchamacallits," he said. "Are they a tribal society?"

"They're not important." She pressed her lips harder to his. This time her tongue slid along the seam of his mouth, running slowly back and forth until he parted his lips to allow her entrance.

His leg pressed lightly against her side. Every part of him ached for more but he forced himself to hold still as he let her be in complete control. She gave a soft moan as he rubbed his tongue along hers.

She shifted her weight and the back of her hand moved from his knee up his inner thigh. The slow journey was torture. He felt as if he couldn't breathe. As she neared the heavy mass of his cock, she leaned over and again whispered in his ear. "What's a lady got to do to get you out of those pants?" The back of her hand rubbed his length through the restrictive material.

"Unfasten them," he answered simply.

She reached to his side and did just that. The pressure of the material released. He felt the blood flow down into his shaft, lifting it even more. He glanced at the door, making sure no one could get in. He saw someone's shoulder, but thankfully no eyes blindly staring toward them. From the way he grew to full length, he wouldn't be able to refasten the constrictive pants until after he found release.

Her eyes closed and her lips parted wide as she reached between his legs to feel his arousal. Her soft, cool fingers wrapped around him. Her breath caught, and he heard a faint, "Holy space balls."

The contrast of light and shadows shifted as she moved.

"What's a lucky guy got to do to get the lady out of those pants?" Jackson turned her words back on her. The light strokes were almost too much. He started to reach to unfasten them for her.

"Wait until the lady offers it," she answered.

He hadn't expected that. Neither did he expect her to shift her weight once again and dip her head downward. His hand hovered by her waist. Her breath hit him seconds before her lips slipped around the tip of his shaft. She began to suck, bobbing her head up and down.

Jackson made a weak noise at the intimate kiss. She moaned in response. He had no idea what he'd done to deserve such a cosmic gift, but he thanked all the alien gods ever dreamt up for it. Her hips moved, as if she was putting off her own desire to give him pleasure.

Just when he thought he might explode, she pulled off and quickly stood. She pushed the pants from her waist, kicking off her shoes as she tried to strip the tight material from her body.

Jackson pushed up from the floor, shoving his pants down his thighs. The second she had one leg free, he grabbed her by her hips, lifted her up, and pressed her back against the stasis chamber wall.

Her dangling pants slapped his leg as they clung to one calf. She held on to to his shoulders, caressing him more than using him for support as he held her easily.

He circled his hips as he tried to find aim. The slick folds of her sex called to him like a beacon, warmer than her mouth had been. The tip of his shaft found what it was looking for and he pushed into her. Her tight body provided a little resistance, and so he slowed.

"Sorry, it's been awhile," she mumbled by way of explanation.

As far as Jackson was concerned, that was nothing to be sorry for. Knowing she didn't take frequent lovers made him feel special. "For me, too."

He couldn't stop himself. He pushed deeper. Blast, but she felt good.

Jackson seated himself to the hilt. She didn't protest as she wiggled against him. Her muscles tightened and released over his shaft. He moved on pure primal instinct, pumping into her. All else faded but the feel of her sex and the sound of her pleasured breathing.

Jackson tightened his stomach and held his release. He needed to feel her climax, needed to watch her face while she did it. He fucked her faster, keeping the thrusts shallow.

"Jack—" Raisa tried to say his name but a tremor cut off her words as she stiffened. Her body clamped down on him.

Jackson pulled out of her, letting her legs fall as he tried to support her. He didn't let himself ejaculate. Her pants still clung to one leg. It took a while for her to catch her breath and she gave him a stunned look.

Her gaze went to his still hard arousal. "Didn't you…?"

"Take your shirt off," he ordered.

She blinked in surprise but obeyed the sexual

command. She kicked the pants away so she stood fully naked before him. He jerked his shirt off, as his body was overheated.

"How do you want it, because I'm going to take you again." He left no room for argument. Of course, if she did argue, he'd respect what she said, but he liked the dominant game they now played.

To his surprise, she pushed away from the wall and knelt before him. Her eyes stayed on his as long as they could while she leaned over onto her hands and knees. She crawled to angle her body down the longer length of the corridor, and then spread her thighs and pushed her ass into the air in offering. She hovered over the light, blocking it so that it outlined her from below, haloing her naked body, shining through the part in her thighs like a signal to his arousal to come home.

Fuck being in control. He'd do whatever she wanted.

Jackson fell to his knees behind her, not caring as the metal floor jarred him on contact. He drew his arousal back to her damp sex and pushed in. He grabbed her breasts from behind, holding them as he worked himself into her body. Her peaked nipples were captured and squeezed between his fingers. The harsh light bounced off the walls as their shadows moved.

He tried to hold back, tried to draw out the

pleasure, but even a highly trained super soldier could only withstand so much torture. The second Raisa began to orgasm, his body responded. He let go of her breasts and pulled her hips down hard against his. His cock pulsed, forcing release from his body as he filled her with his essence. He jerked against her a few more times, giving her every last drop he had.

For a long moment, he couldn't move as he stayed buried inside her. He watched his highlighted cock pull out of her, completely sated. Raisa pushed back, breathing rapidly. She smiled at him, both sated and amazed.

"I can't feel my bones. I think they melted." She gave a small laugh and sat against the wall naked as she tried to regain her composure.

Jackson fastened his pants before moving to sit next to her. She lazily pulled her shirt over her head and reached for the pants. She rolled the back of her head against the wall until she faced him.

"I take back what I said about being bored." She grinned. "This is fun."

Jackson couldn't help himself as he leaned over to kiss her. "As far as being trapped in a secret alien medical facility goes, I'm glad it's with you."

She glanced at the corridor image and he followed her gaze. Dev was gesturing at someone down the hall and waving his hands in irritation. He then looked at the wall before stomping off in the direction he'd shouted.

"Did he just…?" Raisa sprang into action. She leapt up, grabbed her pants and shoes, and his shirt. "Hurry."

The button on the door began to blink. She rushed toward it and began pressing it repeatedly. The door shifted to let them out. Jackson pressed up against her back and they slipped through to the outside corridor before it was completely opened.

12

"Lucien, get your brother out of that hole before he hurts himself," Dev's voice echoed as they came out of the chamber.

"I can't," Lucien answered, not sounding panicked as he added, "he's already stuck."

The chamber door closed. Raisa dropped Jackson's shirt and her shoes on the floor. She rushed to slide her legs into the pants before jumping as she quickly tugged them on. She then took Jackson's shirt and held it out to him as Dev came back around the corner.

"Hey," Raisa asserted, her voice an octave too high as she attempted to act as if nothing was going on.

"They're out," Dev shouted as he strode toward them. The sound of footsteps ran behind him as more of the crew appeared. Only Viktor and Rick were missing.

Jackson took his shirt and pulled it on. As he shoved his head through the neck hole, Lucien, Alexis, and Violette grinned knowingly at him. Dev frowned.

Lochlann chuckled. "Hope we're not interrupting anything." He gave a meaningful nod at Raisa's bare feet. He slapped Dev on the stomach as he strode past the larger man. "I don't think he wanted to be rescued."

"See, Dev, I told you Jackson was fine. He always lands on his feet." Violette threaded her arm through her husband's.

"Or his back," Lucien muttered, though the words were intentionally loud enough for all to hear. He snickered.

Dev turned to him and pointed back the way they'd come. "What are you doing? Get your brother out of that blasted hole!"

Lucien grimaced and saluted before turning to do as ordered. His voice carried back to them as he walked away. "Are we sure we don't want to seal him in there? I mean, I have to ask."

"Well?" Alexis prompted. "What's in there?"

"It is as she said," Jackson answered. "There is a highly advanced, secret laboratory on this ship and it's sucking up a lot of our power."

"Can we shut it off?" Lochlann glanced at the wall. Smears of blood were on it from where the others had attempted to enter but were unsuccessful.

"Possibly, but I don't know if we should," Jackson said. "There are vials of unknown substances. I don't know what will happen if the environment is disturbed, and the laboratory has two subjects. One is long dead, but the other looks to be in hypersleep and might still be alive."

"What do you mean, might? What did the panel for her life functions read?" Lochlann asked.

"It's a language I've never seen before," Jackson admitted. "She could be in stasis or dead."

"She?" Lucien's voice called from around the corner, indicating that he'd stopped to eavesdrop.

"Lucien," Dev warned.

"Fine," Lucien yelled. "I'm going."

"Why didn't you open the door to let me in?" Dev eyed the two lovers with a skeptical lift to his brow.

"That's the thing," Raisa put forth, finally recovering from the slight embarrassment of having what they'd been doing discovered by the crew. "The door doesn't open until this corridor is empty. We had to wait for you to leave so we could come out. And the access panel appears jammed from the inside, so we couldn't leave the way I came in the first time—not that Jackson would fit through the opening or in the repair corridors."

"Well, as curious as this all is, it doesn't provide a solution to our current problems. We need power and we need a propulsion system." Lochlann gave once last glance at the wall and sighed. "No one is to go back in there until it can be properly dealt with as a team. It has been here this long, it can wait."

Footsteps sounded seconds before Rick came around the corner. "What I miss?"

"Alien laboratory," Violette answered.

"Super," Rick said, a little out of breath.

"Why aren't you in the cockpit?" Lochlann asked.

"Like we're going to crawl into an asteroid at the pace we're flying," Rick dismissed. "Besides, communications are down, so I had to come tell you in person. What scans I was able to do of deep space show we have company in the skies. Looks like they might have followed us from Torgan. I can't be sure, but they're coming from that direction."

"The Dokka?" Raisa wondered aloud, fear causing her to panic. "They could be mad that I took my molecular gastro-spectrometer back."

"Federation," Jackson stated.

Though she didn't want to deal with the Dokka again, his answer didn't really set her mind at ease.

Rick nodded. "Could be. The size fits their smaller deep-space vessels."

"You are to turn me over to them," Jackson stated. "I am the one they want. I'll make sure they leave you in peace."

The crew's answers to his suggestion came in unison.

"Stow it," Lochlann ordered.

"No," Dev answered flatly.

"Jackson, come on, be serious," Alexis said, shaking her head.

"Don't be a space cadet," Violette scoffed.

"Will do," Rick agreed. "Never liked you much anyway."

Lochlann frowned at Rick. "Shut your black hole and man the cockpit. We can't outrun them but figure out a way to hide us."

"Aye, aye, spoilsport." Rick could be heard jogging away. "Rick will save the day…once again!"

"What's a spoilsport?" Raisa asked.

"Probably something from twenty-first century Old Earth," Violette said. "Rick's obsessed with that time period. Half the time we don't know what he's going on about."

"Would it be wrong to dose him again to shut him up?" Dev asked. Raisa was surprised the man knew how to make a joke. At least, she assumed it was a joke.

"Out of medicine," Alexis answered.

"I'd be willing to test the alien vials on him," Violette teased. "Could be fun."

"There will be no more dosing of fellow crewmen. Last time someone tied him naked to the dining table," Lochlann said. "We had to sanitize the room for a month before anyone would eat in there again."

Raisa had a feeling this crew joked to hide the fact that they were nervous.

"Why does the Federation want you?" Raisa studied Jackson's face, not joining in the banter. She noticed he liked to avoid any questions related to that part of his past.

"I don't know," Jackson said.

"Really? They just woke up one day and decided to chase you?" Raisa questioned doubtfully.

"A couple of new recruits found him on Torgan while playing with their hand scanner. My guess is they want to reenlist him—" Alexis said.

"They didn't say that," Jackson inserted.

"—but Jackson refused to go with them," Alexis finished.

"They didn't take no for an answer?" Raisa asked.

"They didn't take Jackson's fist in their faces as an answer," Lochlann admitted. "After the Federation soldiers scanned him he was supposed to stay on the ship while we were on the ground so he wouldn't get caught, but for some reason he disobeyed and left. They must have spotted him. Now they're on our trail."

Raisa took a deep breath. Guilt filled her at the realization. "It's because you helped me, isn't it? You left the ship to rescue me and that's why they're coming for you now."

"What's done is done," Jackson dismissed.

"I am so sorry," Raisa said to the crew.

"For what? Needing help?" Violette chuckled wryly. She moved to follow Rick. "If it wasn't this, it would be something else. Life of the high skies."

"Life of the high skies," Alexis agreed.

"I'll help the space cadet in the cockpit. Jackass couldn't fly his way out of a rainbow," Violette said. The soft notes of a pirate song trailed behind her as she sang, "*And we sail the high skies, looking for gold, looking for treasures that never grow old. The wind in our sails, lads, the stars at our feet, as we plunder for women, thick brown, and good mead.*"

"Secret aliens, Federation up our backsides, a broken tin can of a ship." Alexis gave the group a bemused look. "Just another day in space, isn't it?"

Lochlann didn't find the same amusement as his wife. Neither did Dev. Raisa glanced up at Jackson.

And, neither did he.

"Lighten up." Alexis waved her hand at all of

them as if to erase their expressions. She used her husband's arm for leverage as she lifted onto her toes to kiss his jaw. "I'm only teasing. Besides, I wouldn't trade the adventure of being your wife for anything in the known galaxies." She released him and gestured at Raisa. "Grab your shoes and come on. You've had a long day and the security officers need to discuss security stuff. Let's get you something to eat before the real fun starts. I'm dying to know if Jackson actually makes sounds during sex or just stares moodily at a woman in silent disapproval."

"Ah, I, ah…" Raisa stuttered as she looked at Jackson.

His eyes were closed as he grimaced.

Raisa picked up her shoes and moved to follow the woman toward the dining hall.

13

"So, is the alien chick hot, or what?" Rick asked, not taking his eyes off the viewing screen as he maneuvered the slow ship on a new course. The nearest place to hide was on a nearby fueling dock. The hope was that the larger vessel's size would mask their presence to anyone who might be searching for them.

To Jackson's way of thinking, if the Federation did follow them to the fueling dock, it would be the perfect place to turn himself over to the military without endangering his crew. Alexis was probably right. With his training, they probably wanted him to rejoin. He didn't want to go, but this wasn't about him. It was about protecting his family.

Rick turned in his seat when Jackson didn't answer. "You know, you're not a fun guy."

"You're an idiot," Jackson countered. "And, yes, for a blue humanoid woman in stasis for the last countless years that we have flown this ship, she is very pretty."

Rick grinned, winking at him before he turned back to his screen. In a low voice, he murmured, "Oh, yeah. Hot blue alien on board."

Jackson bit back his laugh. He'd never let Rick see he was amused by him. They were alone in the cockpit. Violette had gone for food with Raisa and Alexis. Dev and Lochlann were in the cargo hold looking over inventory they might be able to part with on the fueling dock. Lucien was rescuing his brother from the wall. Well, to be precise, Lucien was *supposed to be* rescuing his brother from the wall.

"You know, I'll deny this if you repeat it, but if this doesn't work and you even dare try to join up with the Federation on this fuel dock, I'll kick your ass. And if they take you, I'm coming to find you." Rick didn't look back as he pushed several buttons on the console before turning a dial.

Jackson appreciated the sentiment. He already knew Rick and the others would try to find him. "You don't expect me to hug you or anything, do you?"

"You're sexy, Jacks, but not my type." Rick laughed. He began to whistle, as if he hadn't a care in the universe. After several minutes, he said,

"You're making me nervous. Go breathe down your lady's neck."

Jackson grumbled a nonverbal answer and left the cockpit. He should have gone to help Lochlann and Dev, but instead found himself standing outside the dining hall door where the women had gone. Alexis and Violette leaned over the table in conversation. At his appearance, they both turned to him.

"I need you to show me this alien language," Alexis said. "I could be searching my database for a match."

"You heard the captain," Jackson denied.

"Since when did any of us obey an order to behave?" Violette dismissed. "Just slip her in there and I'll make sure the corridor stays empty, so you can come back out."

As Alexis walked past him, she hooked his arm to make him go with her. He resisted, and she was unable to move him.

"What if I can save the woman in stasis, and we can shut down the lab safely so that we can power the ship and avoid conscripting you into service?" Her words were logical, and she knew it.

Jackson sighed heavily in response.

Alexis took that as an affirmative to her plan and smiled. "That's more like it."

This time he let her pull him into the corridor. "Where is Raisa?"

"Viktor finally made it out of the wall. He has Raisa looking at the propulsion system." Alexis dropped his arm. "Why? Do we need her blood to get inside?"

"No." Jackson held out his hand. "I need your knife."

Violette reached into her boot and pulled out the weapon. She turned the hilt toward him and handed it over. "We should hurry before Lochlann and Dev finish in the cargo hold."

"Serean. Irrelevant to the situation. Reexamine," Alexis muttered as she searched through her mind for answers. She sat at the dining table, her hands flat on the surface. Her eyes twitched, and she didn't really see what was in front of her. "Syog. Irrelevant to the situation. Reexamine. Feenik. Irrelevant to the situation…"

"Blast the stars," Lochlann swore as he came into the dining hall. "Who sent my wife into a deep search?"

"Shh," Violette hushed him. "I'll tell you if you promise not to get mad."

Jackson averted his gaze. He kept his arms crossed as he stood over Alexis to keep an eye on her progress. The lights flickered, and he heard

Lochlann sigh. He understood the man's frustration. His ship was falling apart around him, and pirates without a ship were, well…dock workers.

"…G'am. Irrelevant…"

Lochlann groaned. He pressed his fingers to a temple and rubbed as if fighting a sudden headache. "You went into the secret lab and she's looking for a way to identify the language."

"… Reexamine. Reticulans…"

"Maybe?" Violette gave the captain a tight smile as she waited to see his reaction.

Lochlann arched a brow at Jackson. "I should have guessed this would happen. Let me know what she figures out."

Violette nodded.

"And you…" Lochlann pointed at Jackson with a stern look. "Check on Viktor in the engine room. See if he needs anything."

"…Brinstoneman…"

Jackson uncrossed his arms and did as he was told. He was eager to see Raisa again, and he quickened his step.

"If we patch the burnt wires and reverse the power supply to that room, we would have more than enough energy to restore the ship to full power," Viktor was saying as Jackson approached the engine room. The lights flickered, as if to punctuate the problem.

Jackson came into the doorway and found Viktor sitting close to Raisa on the floor, his head lowered as they spoke. Metal parts from whatever they were deconstructing were scattered around them in what appeared to be organized chaos.

Raisa nodded. "Agree. Or if we found a way to tap into the reserve."

"Then all we need is to fix this propulsion system," Viktor said. "We could be up and running in a matter of hours."

"We could try welding the cracked casing, but I don't think it will hold for long," Raisa said. She lifted her hand over the metal objects and they rearranged themselves on the floor without her touching them. "I think we can do without the secondary propeller since it's bent and will block airflow—"

Her words stopped when she realized Jackson was watching.

"Lochlann wanted me to see if you needed help with the heavy lifting," Jackson said.

"You have to see this, Jackson," Viktor insisted. "Show him."

Raisa chuckled. She lifted her hands and willed the small parts to move. They slid around the floor.

"Isn't that awesome?" Viktor clapped his hands and rocked back.

"He's easily amused." Raisa dismissed Viktor's

excitement and pushed to her feet. To his surprise, she came to him and lifted up on her toes to give him a kiss. He froze in place, not instantly returning the unexpected affection. She braced her hand on his crossed arms.

Viktor stopped rocking and cleared his throat. He averted his gaze as he reached for a part on the floor.

"What was that for?" Jackson dropped his arms and reached for her before she pulled away.

"Felt like it." She shrugged.

"I see what you mean about the secondary…" Viktor began grabbing parts and rearranging them like a puzzle. "You're a genius."

"You can fix it?" Jackson asked.

"We won't be the fastest ship in the sky, but we'll go," Viktor said. "Give us three hours. We should know then if this will work."

"Possibly two," Raisa said. "We'll do everything we can."

"I'll let Lochlann know." Jackson stopped Raisa from pulling away from him and leaned down to kiss her, harder and deeper than she had him. It was her turn to be surprised.

14

Raisa slammed her hand on the propulsion motor in frustration. She'd gotten used to the lights flickering, though it made her job challenging. "This should have worked."

She had wanted desperately to solve the problem. If they could get power to move through space, they could possibly get away from the Federation vessel following them. Jackson would be safe. She told herself it was because he'd saved her, and she owed him. She also told herself that she knew she wasn't admitting to the full reason.

"It's been four hours," Viktor said, pushing up from the floor and stretching his arms. "Let's step away and prepare to dock. With luck, someone will have the parts we need to do this right."

Raisa arched a brow.

"Long shot, I know," Viktor said.

She liked Viktor. Actually, she liked the entire crew. They were cavalier, and each obviously flawed in their own unique ways, perhaps even damaged by something in their pasts, but they cared for each other and they meant well. Dev was a little scary, but she never felt threatened. Violette had a rough edge to her personality, like she'd been raised in a male-dominated area and had spent her life trying to prove herself. Alexis, well...now that had to be some kind of story, considering the way she could access information just by going into a trance. Lucien and Viktor bickered nonstop, to the point she had to order Lucien to leave so they could work. Lochlann was overprotective, but also a pushover when it came to the will of his wife. Rick could best be described as a devil-may-care flyboy who took nothing seriously and acted like he had nothing and no one to lose.

Then there was Jackson. Just thinking of his touch caused Raisa to shiver. He kept himself guarded. His expressions gave little emotion away. When he stood, his arms were crossed and his stance wide as if someone might try to knock him over at any moment. He also made her feel safe. Something about the challenge he presented made her want to break through the barrier he kept around himself to see what was inside.

"Why are you staring at me?" Viktor asked, touching his face to see if he had anything on it.

"Sorry, I'm drifting." Raisa shook her head and took a deep breath. "It frustrates me when I can't figure out a mechanical or electrical problem."

"Jackson's tough. He'll be fine," Viktor assured her. "We'll keep him safe."

Raisa wasn't sure if Viktor believed that, or if he said it to reassure her.

"Raisa." Lochlann skidded to a stop at the door to the engine room. "Good, you're in here."

"Sorry, Captain, no luck so far," Viktor said.

"We'll keep trying," Raisa added.

"There's no time. It's as we feared. A Federation ship is coming in strong. We've started docking procedures and there's no way we're outrunning them." Lochlann motioned that she should follow him. "There is also no way we're letting them take Jackson."

Raisa hurried to follow him. "Anything I can do."

"We're hiding the both of you in the secret lab. You're not on our roster, and we don't need more questions. We can't deny Jackson was part of the crew, but we'll say he ran off on Torgan. If they can't find him, they can't prove otherwise. You'll have food and bedding, and the rest you'll just have to figure out." Lochlann led the way through the corridors, not slowing. "I don't know how long you'll be in there, but Alexis will be with you. She thinks she's narrowed down a close relative to the alien language. If you can figure out what's happening, I've given Jackson permission to make the call about shutting it down so we can divert power back to the ship. If Viktor can get the engine fixed, we'll be running at full capacity again."

"So, you're going to say Alexis ran off with Jackson?" Even though it was a lie, the idea caused a little pang of jealousy to erupt inside her.

"Alexis is not on the roster and won't be missed. She's, uh…" Lochlann cleared his throat.

"What?"

"People think she's a pleasure droid," Lochlann admitted. "Machines don't need to be registered as part of the crew."

"Alexis is a sex doll?" Raisa gasped. "I wouldn't have guessed. She seems so real."

"She *is* real. She was used as the base model of a pleasure droid line," Lochlann corrected a little gruffly.

Raisa realized she'd hit a sensitive topic. "I didn't mean—"

"It's fine," Lochlann dismissed, though it didn't sound fine.

Raisa wanted to ask more questions but kept them to herself. If Alexis was part machine, that might explain the strange ability she had to sift through great amounts of information like a mental file clerk. "What about the blue alien?"

Lochlann paused and lowered his head. "The lives of this crew come first. Jackson knows that. He'll do what needs to be done."

Raisa realized that meant they could be pulling the plug on Blue. She understood the importance of diverting power to the ship, but if the woman was alive it felt too much like murder.

Lochlann didn't appear to take his decision lightly, and she saw his shoulders slump as he continued to walk.

"This is the last of it," Dev stated, carrying a large crate toward them. "Everything else in the cargo has a slip."

"Drop it off and find your wife. Prepare for docking," Lochlann ordered, as he stepped out of the way to let Dev pass.

Lochlann didn't speak as he led her to the cockpit. Inside, the viewing screen flickered, showing a large metal ship with two bulbous sides joined by a long, skinny center, with grooves cut out of it for ships to dock and fuel. Rick flew *Bound Virgin* with one hand on the controls and the other flat on the console. He artfully maneuvered the ship into place, lining it up to slide into the fueling slot. Raisa grabbed hold of the door frame as they made contact with the metal dock. It jerked her back and forth before the vessel settled into place. Rick began the sequence to cut power to the engines.

"You should get into the room," Lochlann told her. "I'm going to do my best to keep them off the ship. I'll tell them we are a Var vessel and Qurilixen isn't part of the Alliance, and that we don't recognize their authority. It might work, or it might just delay entry for a few days as they convince the authorities on the fueling dock to lock us down until they can look inside."

Raisa nodded, but watched the docking lot for a few moments as connectors reached out to lock the ship into place. The metal clunked as they made contact and it prodded her into action. She went toward the secret chamber. Jackson stood there with Alexis. The pair waited for her. Jackson held a knife.

"We're docked," she said, though her words were probably unnecessary as they would have felt the connectors engage. "The captain wants us to lock ourselves in."

"Any requests from the food simulator?" Alexis asked. "Might be your last chance to get what you want for a few days."

"Whatever you decide is fine." Raisa couldn't think of a single recipe at the moment. A few days? She took a deep breath. Fear trickled into her, an involuntary reaction that filled her chest. What if the Federation searched the ship and found the room? There would be nowhere to run. What if they took Jackson?

"I'll be right back." Alexis jogged down the corridor to retrieve food. Someone had cleaned the blood from the wall and if looked like any regular stretch of corridor.

"We have meal packs if it takes longer than a few days," Jackson said. She guessed he was trying to sound reassuring but being trapped in a secret room didn't sound like fun. "I'm sorry. This situation isn't what I wanted."

At that, she frowned. "Sorry? For what? Saving me from the Dokka? Taking care of me when I couldn't take care of myself? Or for not abandoning me now because there's a little threat of danger from the Federation?"

"Just because *we* didn't know this chamber was here, doesn't mean soldiers with scanners won't find it," Jackson said.

"Got it." Alexis returned with her arms loaded down with food containers. "Let's go."

Jackson nodded and lifted the knife to his hand,

cutting his palm. He placed it on the wall. It recognized him, soaking the blood in and opening.

"Hey, wait," Rick yelled, running toward them with a small box. He stopped, craning his neck to look inside the room. "Whoa."

"Rick!" Lochlann yelled, his voice carrying even though he didn't appear.

"I love you," Alexis called to her husband before stepping inside.

"Wow, thanks. I never knew you felt that way about me, Alexis." Rick grinned, intercepting the words that weren't meant for him.

"Be safe," Lochlann shouted.

Jackson gestured for Raisa to go inside.

Rick shoved a box into Raisa's hands. "Hide this and guard it with your life. The Federation can't get hold of it. It's important."

Raisa nodded. She stepped into the corridor. Jackson joined her, and the door instantly closed to lock them in. Rick stood on the outside and ran his hand over the empty wall before winking at them and blowing a kiss before leaving.

For a long moment, they all stood there. Raisa and Alexis holding their containers, and Jackson with his knife. They stared at the door.

Alexis sighed, breaking the trance. "That kiss was for you, Jackson. *I'm* not taking it."

Raisa laughed despite herself. She braced Rick's

box against her hip to hold it and reached for Jackson's hand. She lifted his bloody palm. "You're still bleeding. Let's wrap this."

Alexis tapped the door, opening it so they could walk into the larger section.

Raisa glanced at the blue woman and frowned. The light was dim, but the woman's hand looked as if it had turned slightly. "Were her fingers like that before?"

Jackson leaned closer to the panel. "You said injectors came out. If she did move, it's probably because the injector's mechanical arm bumped her. Or she was jostled when we synced up to the fueling dock."

"You're probably right," Raisa dismissed. She still held Jackson's hand. Her eyes darted to where they'd made love before. "I'm guessing this stay is going to have to be different than our last one."

Jackson chuckled. "To my great disappointment."

"*Uh-hem.*" Alexis cleared her throat. "I should tell you that I have excellent hearing. And if you two want to get down and freaky, I can go into a search trance."

"Does that work?" Raisa asked.

"No," Jackson answered. "She can still hear everything."

Alexis shrugged and gave a small nod, agreeing

with Jackson. "Yeah, sorry. I tried to help a fellow lady out."

Bedrolls stretched over the floor. Shipping crates had been stacked along one wall. They were stamped with the initials ESC.

"Why do you have crates from the Exploratory Science Commission?" Raisa asked.

"Oh…" Alexis drawled in a low tone as she turned her back and busied herself needlessly with the food.

Jackson didn't avert his gaze, but he also didn't answer.

"Oh, galactic hellfires of Bravon," Raisa swore. "Of course! I'm such an idiot. You're space pirates."

"Good ones," Alexis offered, as if the distinction was important. "Sometimes it takes pirates to keep the so-called legal entities from spreading evil."

"The ESC knows if they leave equipment it is likely to be picked up by travelers," Jackson said. "They actually write it into their budget proposals. It's easier to leave it behind than to cart it back and forth between expeditions."

Alexis stepped too close to the center and the medical chair lifted from the floor. She made a small sound of annoyance.

"That sounds like a justification." Raisa lifted the box from her hip to look inside. Rick had been insistent the Federation couldn't get hold of it.

"It is. But it is also the truth," said Jackson. He examined the cut on his hand.

A low tone sounded in the room. They all stiffened, not moving as they waited to see what would happen. The floating orb came from the wall. It scanned Raisa, then Jackson. A bright stream of light shot out from the orb toward Jackson's hand. He tried to jerk his hand out of the way, but the light followed it. When it turned off, Jackson's hand had stopped bleeding. The orb scanned Alexis, and finding nothing else wrong, retreated into the wall.

"I guess that was nice of it," Raisa said, leaning over to look at his hand. The procedure had left a small line of a scar. "Does it hurt?"

"It burned," he admitted. "Now it's fine."

Raisa poked her finger into Rick's box, pushing around the contents. They were mostly information discs, but there was also a broken handheld unit, and several space chip coins with different planet insignias. She placed the box on top of a crate.

"What now?" Raisa asked.

"We wait," Jackson said. He sat down on a bedroll and glanced up at the wall where the orb was stored. "And occasionally we check the image in the corridor for the all clear."

"I found a region whose language looked close. I'm going to see if I can find anything about the culture which can help me backtrack where else might have been using the dialect in these programs." Alexis dragged her bedroll to a corner of the room and lay down. Moments later, she could be heard mumbling to herself as she sifted through data.

Raisa paced over the short distance a few times before finally sitting by Jackson. "Two seconds into this and I'm already worried about boredom setting in. What are we going to do in here for days?" She studied Alexis' back as the woman faced the wall. Leaning closer to him, she whispered, "Did you know she was a robot? I mean it's remarkable. She looks so real."

"She's not a robot. She is very much human. We rescued her from Pleasure Droid Corporation's test laboratories." Jackson reached into his pocket and took out playing cards. "Kiss My Comet?"

Raisa leaned over and pretended to check out his ass. "Maybe later when we're alone."

"I meant the card game," he corrected with a laugh. "To help with your boredom problem."

"I wouldn't call it a problem. I like to keep my mind occupied." Raisa again turned her attention to Alexis, curiosity still bubbling inside her. "How did she come to be at the pleasure droid test facility?"

"That is her story to tell, if she chooses to tell

it," stated Jackson. He tossed the deck of cards on the ground near the crates.

"They can't just grab women off some planet and put them in a lab," Raisa insisted, keeping her voice low.

Alexis stopped talking to herself and sat up. "My father had a gambling problem. He lost my older sister and then me to the Larceny Casino. They call it 'repossession.' To cover his debts, the casino sold us. She was sold into marriage. I was sold into slavery."

"That's horrible." Raisa pressed her hand to her chest.

"Yes. It is." Alexis pursed her lips together. "I changed hands a few times and ended up as source pleasure droid companion model nine-point-seven. It's easier for them to program their robots if they get their training directly from a live source. They filled me with nanobots, and uploaded millions of files into my brain. It's too much for me to think at once, so I have to wade through it."

"Like when you can't remember a word, but it's right on the tip of your tongue?" Raisa asked.

"Exactly." Alexis nodded.

"So how did you get from there to here?"

"Rick found me and smuggled me out of the facility and this crew saved my life." She started to turn back to the wall. "Turns out the crew was already looking for me. My sister had sent Lochlann to find me. A computer saw my picture, brought my location up as a possible sighting, and here I am."

"So, what about your sister? What happened to her?" Raisa knew she was being nosy, but no one ever accused her of the opposite. She was always prying and asking questions.

"Kendell is married to one of the noblemen from Lochlann's home planet of Qurilixen. She's happy, that's all that matters. But that is a story for another time." Alexis ended the conversation by turning her back to them. She resumed her search.

"That's..." Raisa shook her head. "I can't imagine."

"That's what she was talking about when she said we're good pirates," Jackson said. "We've been flying the high skies for months trying to track down the traders to expose what the Larceny Casino is doing. We had chased down a ship when our electrical blew and we were forced to turn around." He nodded at Alexis and said even quieter, "She did not take the setback well."

Raisa studied Jackson's face as he looked over the alien room. His expressions gave nothing away, except for his rare laugh. The man both amazed and fascinated her. Soldier. Pirate. Vigilante. Crusader. There were so many things she could call him, but none of them seemed to actually define who he was.

"All right. Grab the deck. You might as well teach me this game of yours," she said. "But my version of the game would have been better."

Jackson smiled and nodded as he retrieved the deck.

15

Raisa furrowed her brow as she stared at the puzzle in front of her. The broken handheld in Rick's box of treasures proved to be a challenge. The other crates were food packs, miscellaneous clothing and lab equipment. The broken unit kept her mind busy while Jackson sat in the corridor watching the door, and Alexis went through her strange mental process.

"Mysteries of the Galaxy. A warning guide for space explorers," Alexis said.

Raisa sighed and mouthed along with the woman, "Irrelevant to the situation. Reexamine."

It was becoming a bad song she couldn't get out of her head.

"Irrelevant to the situation. Reexamine."

She had heard of a torture technique that

involved repeating annoying sounds or songs to break the subject's sanity.

"Irrelevant to the situation. Reexamine."

Raisa was there. She was on the edge of saneness. Stress didn't help. Fear didn't help. Isolation didn't help. It was impossible to tell time, but it felt like she'd been in the room for a week. Jackson swore it had only been a couple days. They'd slept on the hard floor. Raisa wasn't a princess who needed a luxury suite, but a white tile floor and thin bedroll had taken their toll on her hips and back. She considered lying on the medical chair, but they had all been avoiding it, afraid lying on it would activate another device.

"Irrelevant to the situation. Reexamine."

"Ahhh," Raisa silently screamed, holding her head as she shook in frustration.

"Irrelevant to the situation. Reexamine."

Grabbing the handheld, she went to the corridor to join Jackson. Alexis didn't move. As she stepped through the door, Jackson looked at her in surprise from the floor.

Raisa gave a humorless laugh, and said, "Irrelevant to the situation. Reexamine."

Jackson chuckled and nodded in understanding. "You get used to it, especially when you see the information she comes up with. That brain of hers has saved our asses more than once."

"I know, she's great. I'm just irritable. I didn't sleep well on that floor, and not knowing what is happening out there is just... Well, you already know this. You know as much as I do." She looked at the image of the corridor. "Anything new?"

Jackson shook his head. "No one has been by. The lights went off for about an hour."

"That's a long time," Raisa observed. She sat next to him on the floor. The reminder of what happened between them in this corridor caused a shiver to work its way over her.

"The power situation could be getting worse." Jackson slid his hand close to hers, letting their pinkies touch.

She closed her eyes, wanting to do more and knowing they shouldn't start. Pulling her hand away, she lifted the device from her lap. "I think I fixed this."

"Really?" Jackson straightened. "Will it turn on?"

"We're about to find out." Raisa pushed on the cracked casing to get it to latch somewhat into place. "It's a face scanner." She lifted it toward his face, and he instantly placed his hand up to stop her.

"Don't."

"But...?"

"It's Federation Military," he said.

Raisa wondered if he was worried that she would find out something about his military career. "It's a manual sync. It has to be docked to get new information. Without a docking port, it's only as good as the information already stored on it."

"So it won't send a signal?" He slowly lowered his hand.

"No." She lifted it toward her face and pushed a button. The unit flashed three times and then she read the output. "See. Subject not identified."

"What does it say about me?" he turned to face her so she could take his picture.

She lifted the unit. It flashed and then instantly, a red indicator light on the top of the unit lit up. She turned the small screen so they could read it at the same time.

"Soldier J-67114, specialized operations. Detain upon contact. Reason classified. Return immediately to Federation class A base. Notation: Subject might be resistant. Highly trained and dangerous. Proceed with caution."

"What is this?" she asked.

"Something I want no part of." Jackson took the unit from her and turned it off.

"This is why the Federation is coming after you? Someone used a unit like this and located you on Torgan, didn't they? And you were safe until I came along."

"They used that unit," he corrected. "I might

have slapped it out of their hands, breaking it, before I…"

"You…?"

"Knocked them unconscious." Jackson averted his gaze toward the blue woman.

Raisa felt there was much in his past he didn't want to talk about, and for some reason she felt no need to pry. She lifted her hand to his stubbled cheek and turned him to face her. Dark circles had formed under his eyes. "You haven't slept, have you? You were up all night watching over us." It wasn't really a question, but a statement. She sighed. "You can't keep doing that. You need to rest. Why don't you lie down and I'll take over watching the door?"

He looked as if he wanted to protest. To cut off his words, she leaned forward and kissed him. It was the first intimate contact they'd allowed since being locked in. The feelings which erupted inside her were hard to contain. There were so many emotions —uncertainty and fear, hope and promise.

Somewhere along the line, she had become invested in Jackson and his crew. Logically, she could have grabbed her molecular gastro-spectrometer, walked off the ship, and found another ride at the fuel dock—one that had a working electrical and propulsion system that wasn't being cobbled together. Yet, she found she couldn't just walk away from them. It never occurred to her that she should leave.

Jackson broke the kiss. His breath heavy, he whispered, "I'll do as you suggest and rest. Wake me if anything happens."

Raisa leaned her head against the wall and waved her hand in dismissal. "Go. Don't worry about us. Blue, Greg, and I have guard duty under control."

16

"I think I found it!" Alexis sat up from her bedroll and grabbed her head. "Whoa. I moved too fast. Everything is spinning."

"That's because you're overdoing it," Jackson scolded. She had been trying to locate the language for the last two days. He had heard her mumbling to herself when she should have been sleeping. Reaching into a crate, he took a meal pack and brought it toward her. "Here. Eat."

"Mmm, nutritional paste in a bag. My favorite," she muttered sarcastically. "Has it only been two days? I thought it was three."

"I lost track," Jackson admitted.

The door to the corridor opened. Raisa motioned frantically for him to come. "Jackson."

Something in her tone made him drop the food

pack and hurry to the corridor.

"Ow," Alexis grumbled as it fell on her.

"They're here. I guess Lochlann couldn't convince the fuel dock authorities to respect the ship's registration." Raisa whispered. The door closed behind him and the holographic display appeared. The corridor was empty.

"I don't see anything," Jackson said. He walked closer and leaned to the side as if that could expand his view farther down the outside hall. It didn't.

"Just watch." Raisa continued to keep her voice low, even though those outside in the ship's corridor wouldn't be able to hear her. An arm in a black sleeve appeared, but the viewing screen flickered off as Alexis opened the door.

Jackson grabbed her arm and tugged her into the corridor so the door would close and the screen would reactivate.

"What is it?" Alexis asked.

An image appeared of a uniformed Federation soldier staring right at them. His black hair was slicked back on his head and his eyes seemed to pierce through the door.

Raisa gasped, taking a step back as she bumped into his chest. Jackson wrapped his arm around her shoulders and held her against him. There had been much he wanted to say to her during their stay in the room, but he had refrained. To act on his feelings for Raisa would have made Alexis uncomfortable, no matter that the woman said she didn't mind. They had managed to steal one quick kiss in the corridor, but Jackson had stopped it. He was tortured enough just being around her, unable to touch her as he wanted, without adding the fuel of her kiss to his fire.

Tension rolled off Jackson as the soldier lifted a handheld scanning device and ran it over the wall. The image flickered and disappeared wherever the bulky unit hovered. Jackson stayed at the ready to shove the women behind him if the soldier made it inside.

"He knows we're here," Alexis came up against his side and grabbed his biceps. Jackson put his other arm around her and pulled her against him. He felt both women tremble and held them a little tighter. He had the same fear but was trained to push it deep inside. This was not the first time he'd been in danger, but it was the first time he'd felt the stakes were this high. If they found the crew hiding him, they would all pay.

The soldier frowned and hit the side of the handheld unit several times. The movement revealed the name on his uniform, "Lang." He again appeared to be looking directly at them before scratching the back of his head and continuing on.

Jackson felt Raisa and Alexis release their

captured breath in relief.

"That was too close," Raisa said.

"He might still come back," Jackson warned.

They huddled together in the corridor, watching as a blond soldier walked past, then one with a bald head, as the Federation searched the ship. Each wore the black uniform of a foot soldier. Jackson determined he could take them in a fight if he had to. At one point, a pair of soldiers pushed Rick down the hall as the pilot tripped in protest. His guards stood about an inch taller than him. One had a scar down the side of his face, and the other bright red hair that hardly looked natural. Jackson automatically looked down at their names, "Hydock" and "Berger."

The pilot kept an easy smile, one that Jackson knew well and had been aggravated by often. Lang joined them, still carrying the scanner. Rick's eyes briefly turned to the hidden door. As Lang began lifting the handheld to the wall, Rick leaned his head back and shouted. Jackson couldn't hear his words, but it was apparently enough to earn him a beating.

Raisa inhaled sharply as the redheaded brute, Berger, punched Rick across the face. The scarred Hydock then aimed for Rick's stomach. Not to be left out, Lang kicked Rick behind the knees so that he fell to the ground.

"We have to do something," Raisa started to move forward to reach for the button to open the door, but hesitated. The corridor's safety precautions wouldn't let them out while people were in the hall.

Jackson knew Rick could fight back, but he took the hits, stumbling and taunting as he tried to lead the soldiers away from the door.

"We can't let them know we're in here," Alexis whispered.

Rick's head was slammed against the metal wall in front of the door. The screen showed it as detailed as if he'd smashed against a window. Raisa yelped and turned away. She pressed her face into Jackson's chest.

Blood smeared the outside wall. Thankfully, the room didn't recognize Rick's blood and stayed closed. Rick crumpled to the ground. Hydock kicked him in the gut one last time before they left him on the corridor floor to continue their search. He could see them laughing at what they had done.

"Is it over?" Raisa lifted her head up to peek.

Rick weakly pushed himself up to sit against the wall. Blood trickled from his scalp and nose, trailing down the side of his face and covering his chin. He wouldn't have been able to see out of his swollen left eye. He grabbed his stomach and grimaced.

Then, holding up his free hand, he gestured

with his thumb in the air and gave them a pained smile.

"Blasted spaceholes, Rick," Alexis swore under her breath. "You crazy bastard."

Jackson knew Rick was the only reason the man with the scanner hadn't found them. The pilot slumped against the wall and closed his eyes. More soldiers came by brandishing weapons. They stepped over Rick, not bothering to help him up.

Dev appeared carrying a large metal box. It seemed to be filled with pieces of silk, beads, and other treasures from the cargo hold. They were all obtained legally as gifts from the royal family on Lintian. The soldiers had no right to it. Still, they held Dev at laser point and forced him to carry their bounty toward the entry hatch.

"Can they do this?" asked Raisa.

"They can do whatever they want, and they know it," Alexis answered.

"Maybe we can open the door and grab Rick before anyone sees," Raisa suggested.

"No. They'll notice he's missing and he'll have taken that beating for nothing." Jackson hated seeing him injured, but the wounds did not appear to be serious.

"Lochlann will make sure he gets treatment," Alexis said, though he heard the fear in her voice. She worried for her husband.

None of them moved as they watched the screen. Only the sound of their breathing filled the small space. Finally, after what felt like an eternity, Dev returned. He glanced over his shoulder, before holding up both hands and pressing them down and forward to signal to Jackson to stay put. Then, going to Rick, he lifted the man into his arms and carried him away.

"I hate not knowing what's happening out there," Alexis whispered.

"Lochlann knows how to take care of himself," Jackson assured her. Alexis pushed away from his side and he released his hold. Raisa was slower to pull back. "What we *can* do is figure out what these monitors are saying." He turned Raisa toward the inner door and touched it so that it would let them in. "The biggest help we can be is to fix the power on this ship."

"And save that poor woman," Raisa added.

"Yes, and save the woman," Jackson agreed. He appreciated Raisa's compassion for the sleeping stranger. No one wanted to pull the plug on the stasis chamber, but if this ship became powerless in the middle of deep space, it would not only kill the crew, it would kill the woman as well. Tough decisions would have to be made.

17

"It's an old Hungariz dialect," Alexis explained. "From what I can tell, it's pretty obscure. The people who used it disappeared from their settlements almost overnight. It's quite the mystery. I think I was able to access enough of it to figure out what it's saying though."

"What kind of people were they?" Jackson walked around the medical chair. Raisa followed him.

"Peaceful from what I can tell. There was no mention of wars or galactic trouble. They were secretive, but that's really nothing special in the universes. Many people choose to keep to themselves." Alexis went to the floating panel by the medical chair.

"They were clearly educated and technologically

advanced." Raisa gestured around the room to prove her point.

Alexis glanced toward the exit. Raisa knew she was worried about her husband. Jackson placed a hand on her shoulder. Alexis nodded in silent understanding.

"This looks like a menu." Alexis studied the hologram. "To unlock, we have to draw a circle on the screen three times. I think it's to ensure that only people who read the language know how to get in." She drew three circles, and a new list appeared. "Log. Food, maybe. Medical. Diagnostics. And I don't know the last one."

"Try log." Jackson gestured that she should touch the screen.

Alexis reached up and pushed the button. They watched the screen. A strange sound came from behind and they turned to see the image of a holographic man sitting on a chair at the metal table. The sound was his voice, speaking in a rapid wave of tonal sounds. He was humanoid. His transparent image gave the impression of blue-tinted skin, not as deep as the woman in stasis, but close. Age had done its march across his wrinkled features. His hands looked emaciated. Light, thin hair pulled into a peak down his forehead.

"Can you translate it?" Jackson asked.

"Can you make him speak the star language?" Raisa stepped closer to study the man's face.

"Shh." Alexis waved her hand to get them to be quiet. She narrowed her eyes as she listened. "His town was attacked, most died, those who survived were sick. His wife survived. She was ill. He worked on a cure. Built this chamber. Made deal with Kintoks. Something about blood locks."

"The door," Raisa whispered. Jackson nodded.

"Intense hunger. Feeding tubes installed. Transfusion worked. Wife suspended in hypersleep. He can't take care of her. Hopes someone will come along to wake her." Alexis looked at them as the hologram stopped.

"What about Greg?" Raisa asked. "Any word on who he was and why he's floating in dark goo?"

"He didn't say," Alexis answered. "That's all I could understand. I'll try to access more of the language, but I'll need time."

"So, we can wake her up?" Raisa assumed. "He said he left her so that someone could wake her. He looked old. Maybe he knew his time was limited."

"Are there any more files?" Jackson turned to the screen and touched the log button. The same recording began.

"I think that's it." Alexis pushed the third button on the screen and began to read. She flicked her fingers several times to scroll through the data presented. Then, she went to the drawers of medicines. She tapped one to open up the inventory. "These are all medications. I think they're for our friend in there. The computer analyzes what she needs and then gives it to her. It's automated."

"Unless you manually administer something," Raisa inserted, remembering how she'd accidentally pushed a button for *Grarf.*

"Yes." Alexis went back to the main screen. "The combination to wake her up is in here. All I'll need to do is press the symbols. The system should do the rest and administer the right medicines."

"So this chair is probably for her," Raisa guessed. She placed her hand on the medical chair. Nothing happened. The cushioned padding felt better than anything else they had to sit on. "Is this safe?"

"I think so?" Alexis didn't sound sure.

Raisa hopped up to sit on it. She waited to see if anything activated. It didn't.

"Try diagnostics," Jackson said.

Alexis pushed a button. Large diagrams of the room came up, spreading from the monitor parallel with the floor. "It's a floor plan. Maybe the word meant schematics?"

"Why did the computer log us in when we called to it? That's a star language command," Raisa said.

"Could be voice tone, or the fact the word

sounds close to the Hungariz word for archive."
Alexis pushed the map around in the air with her
finger.

"Can you slide the map this way?" Raisa asked.
Alexis lifted her hand and motioned toward Raisa.
The diagram moved toward her.

Raisa lay back on the chair to look up at it. The
cushioned seat was surprisingly comfortable, and
she felt foolish for not trying it before. It was the
most relief her sore hips and back had felt in days.
They'd been so cautious about activating anything.
"Now *this* I understand." She reached up, motioning
her hand to get the diagram to turn. She pointed to
a square outlined behind the wall beneath the orb.
"That looks like the power reserve. If we push the
tile, it should open up and we can plug in to it if we
find the right adaptor." She traced the wires around
the room, zooming in as she figured out how the
system was set up. Seeing a small rectangle with a
zigzag pattern on it, she said, "And that would be
where we find access to the second grid to stop it
from syphoning power from the rest of the ship. If I
disconnect that, Viktor will have the energy he
needs and then some. Looks like we pull a fuse and
yank a wire."

"That's great news," Alexis said.

Raisa continued examining the plans. The
medicine drawers were connected to both the stasis

chamber and the tank. "Any idea what kind of alien Greg is?"

"Sea creature of some kind?" Alexis touched the monitor and the diagram disappeared. After a while of searching, she shook her head. "I can't find anything. Unless this button doesn't say 'Food,' like I first thought."

Raisa pushed up from the chair. "Can I see the diagram again?"

Alexis obliged.

Raisa lay back down and looked at the chambers. "It's almost like they're connected to each other. Maybe Greg was part of the cure?"

"Try the food button." Jackson crossed his arms over his chest and looked at the monitor. Alexis pushed the button. The diagram went away, and they waited for a new screen to appear.

Raisa felt something move by her ankles. She braced her hands and pushed up. Jerking her leg, she realized it was locked into place. Movement by her wrists pulled her arms down and locked them on the bed.

Raisa released a high-pitched sound of fear as she was forced to lay flat. "Jackson!"

Something clamped her waist, and the bed lifted up from the floor closer to the ceiling. She thrashed, trying to free herself. Jackson leapt up, grabbing hold of her arm and the bed as he tried to free her.

"Stop it!" Jackson yelled.

"I'm trying," Alexis replied.

Raisa screamed, trying to jerk all her limbs at once. The ceiling opened. Jackson lost his hold and fell back. Several large injectors came down, aiming for her thighs and neck. Tears streamed down her temples. "Oh, please help me, Jackson..." She screamed. Two injectors stopped moving and hovered over her, but the third needle pierced her thigh. Clicks sounded. Fluid came down a tube and she felt a burning sensation in her leg.

Jackson leapt up, grabbed hold of the bed by her waist, and pulled his body weight up until he could brace his knees by her legs. He grabbed the injector and pulled. His muscles strained, and he cried out as he tried to remove it from her. The injector filled with red as it drew blood from the same injection site.

Alexis yelled commands from below, but Raisa couldn't hear them as she cried out in pain. Liquid fire spread over her body, carried in her bloodstream.

He paused, punching the side of his hand against one of the hovering injectors, breaking it off, only to resume pulling. He then hit the injector by her neck. It took a couple strikes with the side of his arm before the needle receptacle bent to the side. His blood dripped on her cheek from the effort. He stood, his neck hitting the ceiling. Raisa watched him move over her. Her vision swam and she felt lightheaded.

"Cut the tube," Alexis yelled.

Jackson let go of the injector arm and jerked the tubing leading to it. After several hard tugs, it came free. Blood sprayed over her, the ceiling, and Jackson. A grinding sound came from above and the needle finally retracted from her leg.

"*Sacre,*" Alexis swore. "What was that?"

Jackson pressed his hands to Raisa's wound. "Get these restraints off her." The bed started to lower. "Whatever you're doing is working."

"I'm not doing that," Alexis said. "The computer locked me out."

Raisa felt the restraints release. She reached for Jackson, grabbing his shirt. "Get me off this."

Jackson hopped from the bed and pulled her into his arms. He carried her across the room to the crates and sat on the floor, still holding her close. She didn't fight his embrace. A chill settled over her, causing her to shake. Her head was light, and she found a small comfort, resting against his chest.

18

"What did that machine do to her?" Jackson rocked Raisa on his lap, holding her tighter. She mumbled incoherently, and her eyelids drifted closed. Blood marred his hands. It stained her face and neck. "We need to get her out of here. She needs a medical booth."

"We have to turn off the power to this room." Alexis lifted her arms, helplessly. "Which means we have to decide what to do about Blue. Do we wake her or kill her?"

Jackson knew it was on his shoulders to make a decision. He had seen so much death during his service. He didn't want to kill again, not unless he had reason. The blue woman had given them no reason.

"Her husband said she was cured?" Jackson asked for confirmation, his words rushed.

"He said the transfusion worked," Alexis corrected. "You could interpret that as she is cured. But another way to look at it would be that this place, as advanced as it is, was set up a long time ago. Medical booths have come so far, more diseases categorized. We could put her in it when she wakes up and run a diagnostic on her."

Raisa convulsed in his arms.

"We don't have time to debate. Wake Blue up and shut this room down." Jackson lifted Raisa in his arms. "This crew has never condemned anyone to death without cause, and we won't do so now."

"We don't know if it's clear from the Federation out there." Alexis turned to the monitor and took a deep breath. Blood covered the medical chair.

"I'm not losing her, Alexis." Jackson held Raisa against him, adjusting her weight in his arms.

Alexis nodded, not offering any more warnings. "Get Raisa by the exit."

Jackson carried Raisa toward the small corridor. She hung limp in his arms.

"I'm waking Blue up." Alexis pushed a series of buttons. "As soon as I finish this sequence, I'll pull the fuse. This room will run on reserve power until that runs out."

Jackson waited impatiently, holding the door open for Alexis. "Hurry."

A hiss sounded by Blue. Needles reached toward her from all directions. Her body bounced as electricity shot from the sides of the unit. Her coloring had changed, not as deep blue as before. Tinges of pink had started appearing around her nose and eyes.

"Is it working?" Alexis called.

"Something is happening." Jackson wasn't sure how this stasis chamber worked but had to assume it was doing what it was supposed to.

"Is the corridor clear?" she asked.

Jackson let the door close and the corridor image came up, showing no one was outside. He again opened the door to Alexis. "Let's go."

"Pulling the power fuse," Alexis said. The sound of kicking was followed by a loud grunt of exertion. The power flickered for a few seconds but came back on as it switched over to the reserve. "Got it!"

"Come on," Jackson ordered.

Alexis hurried to him. She dropped the fuse on the floor. "Let's go."

Jackson glanced at the woman in the chamber. The syringes still injected into her. Steam misted over Blue from above, obscuring her.

"We'll come back to check on her. This process might take a while." Alexis let the door shut and as soon as the corridor image appeared, she pushed the blinking button to open it. To the woman, she said, "Good luck, Blue."

Jackson looked out of the corridor. The lights were flickering, but brighter than before. The power diversion seemed to be working just like Raisa said it would. He listened for footsteps. Not hearing any, he ran as lightly as he could toward the medical booth. Raisa didn't move in his arms. She didn't moan or indicate she knew what happened around her.

Jackson felt as if he couldn't breathe. He paused at a corner to listen.

Alexis grabbed his arm. "Let me lead."

He nodded. She stepped around the corner and motioned him to follow. She ran ahead of him, leading him down another corridor. She stopped at the small room holding the ship's medical booth. The lights turned on at her presence. "Get her inside."

Alexis stood guard at the door as Jackson placed Raisa in the medical booth and closed the lid to lock her in so she didn't slide down from the angled, upright position of the booth. Her head was exposed so he could watch her for movement.

Jackson went to the console and activated the device. It automatically tried to focus on her healing ribs, but he overrode the directive. Instead he made it analyze her blood.

"Someone is in the corridors," Alexis whispered. "I hear footsteps."

Jackson alternated between staring at Raisa's motionless face and the console. The results appeared, and he kept his voice quiet as he said, "It injected her with some kind of enzyme."

Alexis stepped back into the room. Her voice soft, she said, "Medical booth protocol. Relevant to situation. Humanoid. Circulatory system. Blood additives. Clean." She blinked several times, coming out of her trance as she hurried to the booth. She began pushing buttons at a rapid rate as she programmed the unit to override the automatic functions. Lasers lit over Raisa's body, illuminating her face with a green light.

Jackson hurried to the door and peeked out. He too heard footsteps in the corridor. They didn't appear to be moving quickly, but they did appear to be approaching. He concentrated on the pattern of the steps "Someone is coming. It doesn't sound like one of us."

"It's working," Alexis said. "The second it's done, get her out of there and hide."

"What are you going to do?" Jackson asked, not liking the look on Alexis' face.

"What I'm programmed to." She took a deep breath, changed her posture, and stepped into the corridor. Jackson watched her, torn between pulling her back into the room, and protecting Raisa. He trusted Alexis knew what she was doing.

"Hello. Welcome." The docile tone of Alexis' voice sounded odd, and a little too high pitched. She moved with a deliberate stiffness as she turned out of his eye line. "I am Alexis, pleasure droid companion model nine-point-seven."

"Whoa, check that thing out," a deep voice said. "Honar, come here."

A second set of footfalls sounded. "Arte, this better be something. This place is a hellhole."

Jackson willed the unit to hurry. He could hide Raisa behind the booth where she couldn't be seen from the outside hall and then help Alexis.

"Look," Arte said. "They got one of those pleasure dolls."

"How in the galaxies do a bunch of drifters afford something like that? They can't even keep their lights from flickering in this tin can," Honar said. "Hey, you, who is your controller."

"Her name is Alexis," Arte inserted.

"I belong to the captain." Alexis managed to keep her voice calm. "Please, it is my duty as hostess to offer refreshments. Let me escort you."

Jackson stayed as quiet as he could, as Alexis tried to lure the soldiers away.

"Alexis, lift your shirt for me," Arte ordered.

Jackson's eyes narrowed, and his fists tightened.

"What are you doing?" Honar asked.

"I want to see how real she is," Arte answered.

"Warning," Alexis said, her tone changing. "I belong to Captain Lochlann, of the ship *Bound Virgin*. Any attempts to remove me from the ship or tamper with my program directives will result in a self-destruct that will harm those within my immediate vicinity."

"Leave it alone," Honar said. "I heard they can blow a man's penis off if you mess with a doll that's not yours."

"That's just an old ship tale," Arte dismissed.

Raisa moaned softly, her head turning. The medical booth was working.

"Shh," Jackson whispered into her ear. She blinked, not seeming to focus her vision as she looked around in confusion.

"Unhand me." Alexis' tone changed.

"She feels real," Arte said.

Jackson sprang into action. He came out of the medical booth room. "You heard her."

"Blast, it's him!" Honar cried.

Arte had Alexis pressed up against a wall, his hand on her shirt. He tossed her at Jackson and reached for a blaster on his waist.

Jackson caught Alexis and pushed her into the room with Raisa, and out of harm's way.

"We're going to get a stripe for this one," Honar said in excitement, also pulling a blaster pistol.

"I will give you one chance to leave," Jackson said, hoping they'd take the opportunity yet knowing they wouldn't.

"The Federation doesn't enlist cowards," Arte denied.

Jackson frowned. "Do you even know who you are chasing?"

"Pirate scum," Honar blustered.

Jackson stood ready to defend himself. He glanced to the side. Alexis was pulling Raisa from the booth. She looked dazed, but alive.

When he glanced back, he tensed in surprise.

Blue stood in the corridor. Her shimmering gown hung around her thin body. Her long brown hair framed her beautiful face as it fell to her waist. She tilted her head one direction and then the other, as if trying to assess what was happening. Her movements were jerky and strange. He willed her to hide.

Before Jackson could disarm his captors, Blue lurched her body forward. She ran barefoot toward the soldiers. At the sound, the men turned.

Her yell sounded half human, half screech. She slashed her hand, cutting Honar's neck, before she latched her teeth into Arte's throat. Blood sprayed over the corridor, staining her gown and pooling on the floor.

Arte thrashed about in shock. Yelling as he tried to throw the surprisingly agile woman off him.

Alexis appeared in the doorway. Raisa swayed groggily behind her. Jackson backed away from Blue and motioned that they should get behind him. Arte fell to his knees, no longer screaming.

"Run," he ordered the women quietly.

Raisa grabbed hold of his arm and he met her eyes briefly. She looked like she had a hard time standing. Alexis pulled on her arm. They weren't moving fast enough.

Blue's eyes lifted as she unlatched her mouth. They swam with the color of blood. Her features had filled out, as if the blood gave her health.

Jackson turned and rushed a few steps to catch up with the women. He lifted Raisa over his shoulder like the first day they'd met and ran with her down the corridor. He heard bare feet chasing them, recognizing the dull slap of skin to metal. For a woman who just woke from a deep sleep, she moved with surprising dexterity.

Alexis led the way into the captain's quarter and slammed her hand against the door scanner, instructing the door to lock.

"Computer, show security footage from outside

this room," Jackson ordered, as he lowered Raisa to her feet.

"Yes, Grumpy Warrior," the computer answered. Alexis went to the viewing area behind the cage.

Jackson studied Raisa's face. She blinked slowly and he could tell she was fighting to stay upright. "Is she going to be all right?"

"Yes, the booth cleaned the enzyme from her blood, but she'll be weak from the blood loss," Alexis answered.

"I'm fine," Raisa insisted.

Jackson pulled her close. The fear of what had almost happened hitting him. "I can't lose you."

"Then let go of me and let's see what this blood-drinking banshee is doing," Raisa answered, pushing at his chest. "You can hold me after we save the ship and then say all the sweet things I want to hear."

He couldn't help the half smile that twitched the sides of his lips. "It's a promise."

"What in all the galaxies did we wake up?" Alexis asked.

They joined her behind the couches to look at the screen. Blue stood close to the door, her head moving slowly back and forth like a predator trying to smell through the metal barrier. Her hand lifted, and she silently pet the frame with her long nails.

"I'm starting to rethink my stance on waking Blue from hypersleep," Raisa mumbled. "Alexis, do you know what kind of alien that is?"

"The doctor's recording didn't say anything about his wife being a psycho blood hunter." Alexis took a deep breath.

"We should get on the comms and try to warn the rest of the crew," said Raisa. "If they're on board, they need to hide. If they're not, they need to stay off and lock the hatches. She can't be allowed onto the fueling dock."

"I have no idea how we're going to explain the two dead soldiers in the corridor," Alexa said.

"What is she doing?" Jackson frowned at the screen as Blue walked her fingers slowly upward before turning to look at the camera. She appeared more intelligent than a mindless creature searching for food. "Raisa's right. We need to warn the others."

"Computer, locate the members of the crew," Alexis ordered.

"Yes, Captain's Boss," the computer answered. "Locating. Life signs are detected in the cargo hold—Crewmember Angry Pants, Captain Please-let-us-go-to-the-Galaxy-Playmates-show, Crewmember Beautiful, with unknown entities. Life signs detected in the cockpit—Pilot Rocket Boy with unknown entity. Life signs detected in the engine room—

Crewmember Lady's Magnet, Crewmember Victorious Lord. Life signs detected in the corridor—unknown entity."

If they made it out of this, Jackson was going to have words with Viktor and Lucien about their programming jokes. Angry Pants had to be Dev. So Dev, Lochlann, and Violette were in the cargo hold. Rick was in the cockpit with soldiers. Lucien and Viktor were in the engine room.

Raisa counted out the names on her fingers. "They're all on the ship." She grabbed hold of his arm.

"And they're not alone. It's only a matter of time before the Federation soldiers stumble across the dead bodies," Jackson added.

"Or worse, *her*." Raisa let go of his arm. "Computer, contact Rick."

"Please state your identity," the computer answered.

"Computer, input Raisa. Full command."

"Yes, Captain's Boss."

Computers were useful, but sometimes they were a pain in the backside. They had no sense of urgency.

"Computer, connect me to Rick," Raisa said. Lower, to Jackson, she added, "We need to see if he's all right after that beating."

"This is handsome Commander Rick of the

Bound Virgin, standing with Space Cadet One and Black Hole Two," Rick's voice answered, the connection filled with static. He sounded as if he had no care in the galaxies. Jackson suspected that wasn't the case.

"Rick," she answered. "You need to lock yourself in the cockpit."

"What's that, baby cakes?" Rick asked. "I'm sorry, I can't play games with you right now. I'm entertaining guests."

"We have a visitor, and she's not looking for a date," Alexis interrupted.

"Rick, stasis lady is up and she's drinking blood. Get your ass to safety," Jackson ordered. They didn't have time to try to send coded messages. Ship safety had always been his concern, and right now the Federation might help. "Computer, connect us to Lochlann."

"This is the captain," Lochlann sounded hesitant. "I think there has been an error in the computer coding. No one unaccounted for is on the ship. Computer, reset your system."

"No!" Jackson and Alexis yelled at the same time.

"Lochlann, danger, ru—" Alexis yelled through the computer comm system at her husband.

"Attention crew. All systems reset. Goodbye." The computer cut her off.

Blue smiled at the camera. It would have been a pretty look if blood didn't stain her chin. Suddenly, her head whipped to the side and she stared down the corridor. Seconds later, she pushed away from the door and ran. The viewing screen went dark as the computer reset its functions.

"Computer, connect me to Lochlann," Alexis demanded. The computer didn't respond. "Computer!"

"Stay here," Jackson ordered. "I'll find the others. Figure out what in the blazes that thing is and how we stop it." He unlocked the door and waited as it slid open. "Lock this behind me."

"Remember your promise." Raisa lifted her hand, shutting the door behind him.

19

Raisa took a deep breath and didn't turn away from the door. "Are you ready to go? I say we give him thirty more seconds before we follow."

Jackson would have argued if she'd told him she wasn't going to sit in the captain's quarters while everyone else was in danger. She'd advocated to wake Blue from stasis. This was on her as much as it was on the other two.

"How did you know I wasn't staying put?" Alexis joined her by the door.

"Because your husband is out there." Raisa saw the love Alexis had for Lochlann. It was the same way she felt when she looked at Jackson. His nearness made all the craziness happening around them seem right. It made spending days locked in a secret alien medical chamber seem like the thing to do. It made running after a neck-drinking devil woman seem rational.

"And why are you going?"

Raisa glanced briefly in her direction and then away.

"I suspected as much," Alexis said, clearly guessing Raisa's true reason. "You chose well. Jackson is a good man."

Alexis handed her a blue scarf. At Raisa's questioning look, the woman wrapped a green scarf around her own neck and said, "Hey, protection couldn't hurt. That banshee has bite."

"How do we stop her?" Raisa asked, hoping the woman would have the answer somewhere inside her fantastic brain. She wrapped the material several times to cover her throat.

"Luck." Alexis lifted her hand to the scanner, looked at Raisa, who nodded that she was ready, and then opened the door.

The sound of the sliding metal felt ominous. Fear crept into her stomach, and her hands shook as they stepped into the corridor. Of course she was frightened. That she-creature was terrifying.

"If you see something you can use as a weapon, grab it," Alexis instructed.

They stayed close to the wall as they crept down the corridor. The silence made every brush of her arm, hitch in her breath, and step of her foot sound like a dinner bell. The lights flickered and they both stopped. The corridor lit with a subdued red. Raisa really hoped that was the computer resetting the electrical system. She also hoped that it would be done soon.

Though they walked quickly, each leg of their journey felt like an eternity. They turned the corridors, leading the way toward the back of the ship. Finally, Alexis stopped and lifted her hand. The sound of voices could be heard coming from nearby.

"I have explained this ship has power issues. That's why we were looking for parts on Torgan, and why we docked here." Lochlann sounded annoyed. "As a courtesy, I have allowed you to search every inch of this ship multiple times. The man you are looking for is not here and our cargo checks out. Given that this ship is registered to the royal family on Qurilixen, we aren't under Federation jurisdiction and are not required to cooperate further. I request that you let us carry on with our repairs, or I will be forced to file a complaint with the Qurilixen reigning family."

Jackson clearly had not gone in there. And, since there was no screaming, she could assume Blue also hadn't wandered in.

Raisa touched Alexis' arm to get her attention

and motioned that she was going to find Viktor and Lucien to warn them.

Alexis hesitated a moment before nodding. She then straightened her shoulders and walked stiffly toward the cargo bay. "Hello. Welcome." Alexis' gentle voice drifted. "I am Alexis, pleasure droid companion model nine-point-seven."

Raisa didn't wait to hear more. She took a deep breath, mustering the courage to go on alone. The heavy clank of striking metal rang from the engine room.

"Who the hellfires is that?" Viktor yelled. Metal stuck again, then the sound of skidding as if a tool slid over the grated floor.

Lucien cried out, "Get off me!"

Raisa wished for a weapon. She knelt close to the floor and slowly peeked in.

Blue held on to Lucien as he thrashed to escape. Lucien screamed. Blue's back was turned toward the entryway as Viktor threw tools at their attacker in an effort to force her to release his brother.

A wrench slid close to the door. Part of her wanted to run away and hide. But then she thought of Jackson's face as he'd gone into danger. She thought of how he'd saved her life. How he loved this crew. Flashes of memories filled her—Blue in stasis, the blood covering the halls as the soldiers died, the fear of being buried alive in the desert.

Raisa leapt into the engine room before she lost her nerve. She reached down to grab the wrench, only to come up swinging.

Blue spun around. Blood covered Lucien's throat. Blue tossed the man aside and he crumpled on the ground.

Raisa swung, hitting Blue across the side of the face. The woman stumbled but absorbed the blow as she regained her footing.

Blue smiled, as if she'd enjoyed it.

"You can't do this," Raisa said, her voice shaky as she tried to reason with the woman. She held the wrench before her with two hands, wielding the weapon for protection. "I know things are different than you remember, but we don't want to hurt you. Please don't make us. We will defend ourselves."

Viktor grabbed hold of his brother's hand and dragged him behind an engine block. "Get out of there, Raisa!"

"It must be very confusing coming out of stasis," Raisa continued, forcing her words to be calming and soft.

"I don't think she can understand you," Viktor insisted.

"I..." Blue answered, as if the star language words were hard to form. "I know what this place is."

"Yes, it's a ship." Raisa nodded in encouragement. "Your husband put you in stasis. We woke you up."

"Ship," Blue repeated. "Hus. Band."

"The doctor, your husband. He said he found a cure," Raisa said. "I'm sorry, but I don't think he's still alive."

"Weak. Hus. Band. Airlock." Blue made two fists and then expanded her fingers, spreading her hands apart as if to signify a blast.

"He threw himself out of an airlock? I'm sorry." Raisa didn't let go of the wrench. Instead she lowered it to her side. "You are safe on this ship."

"I know what this place is," Blue repeated. Her smile returned. "Feeding ground. You are not safe."

The woman darted forward. Raisa swung.

Blue didn't seem to feel pain as the wrench made contact with her arm. Her shoulder dropped back only to instantly recover. Her mouth opened, and multiple fangs extended down from her gums to create a mouthful of sharp teeth.

A strong hand grabbed hold of Raisa's wrist before she could swing another time. Blue tried to bite, but her teeth snagged on the scarf and she pulled away. The material yanked at Raisa's neck and they both stumbled.

Raisa pushed toward Blue as hard as she could, throwing her weight against the woman. Blue fell onto her back. As Raisa landed on top of her, Blue's mouth pulled free from the scarf. They wrestled on the floor. The scarf fell away.

"Get him out of here," Raisa ordered Viktor.

"I'm not leaving you!" Viktor denied.

"Medical booth is on," Raisa insisted, grunting as Blue slammed her forehead into Raisa's jaw.

Viktor appeared next to them. "Move."

Blue released her wrist and grabbed both sides of her face. Raisa drew the wrench up, shoving it between Blue's teeth to stop the bite.

Blue's screech covered the sound of cracking teeth. Her grip loosened.

Viktor grabbed Raisa's arm and jerked her back. She slid along the floor in his wake.

Blue pushed to her knees and grabbed her throat as if she'd inhaled the broken fangs. When she gasped for breath, her mouth opened to show jagged, chipped teeth.

"Get your brother to the booth," Raisa ordered.

This time Viktor listened to her and went to help Lucien to his feet. "Raisa, come on, get out of here."

Blue coughed. Tiny droplets of dark green sprayed from her lips. She glared at Raisa, trying to crawl toward her. The woman made a horrible gurgling noise.

"Hold it," someone yelled behind her.

"In there," Viktor answered. "Hurry."

Raisa pushed her heels into the floor to get away. Two soldiers appeared next to her. She recognized them as two who'd beaten Rick—Hydock and Lang. At first, Lang pointed his blaster at her, but seeing Blue, it became obvious who the aggressor was, and he changed his target.

Lang tried to ask, his shock evident, "What is—"

Blue screeched, cutting off his words.

"Shut your black hole!" Hydock lifted his blaster and fired.

Blue absorbed the pulse and kept crawling.

He shot her again.

Raisa felt heat on her arm and looked down to see blood staining her shirt. Blue's nails had cut her.

The blaster didn't seem to effect Blue. She coughed and grabbed her throat before falling face first onto the floor, choking and gurgling until she stopped breathing.

"I got her," Hydock bragged.

Raisa glared at the man's back, wanting to hit him. Her hand balled into a fist. It took all of her willpower to say, "She killed two other soldiers. You'll probably get a medal for taking her down."

The men gave shouts of excitement.

"We won't just get medals, we'll get a stripe for this mission," Lang exclaimed.

"Bagged a monster and captured a fugitive," Hydock boasted.

Lang nudged Blue with his boot and laughed.

"Fugitive?" Raisa asked, her voice too soft for them to hear. That could only mean one thing. They had Jackson. She backed away from the soldiers and ran down the corridor.

20

A t least the Federation was off their ship.

Jackson watched as they loaded Blue's dead body onto a transport next to him. Relief filled him to know someone had stopped the woman from escaping the ship and doing more damage. He had no doubt that if a creature like her was let loose, she'd not stop her attacks on her own. That relief was quickly replaced by worry as he wondered who else Blue had harmed.

Thick manacles covered his wrists, holding them crossed in front of him. He tried pulling free, but they were magnetized to a belt around his waist and all he managed to do was cut the base of this thumb. Matching bracelets wound around his ankles, locking his feet against a platform. The prison disc kept him hovered over the ground so they could easily push him where they needed him, like cargo.

Dodson, a blond soldier, walked by and purposefully tapped Jackson's arm to send him into slow rotation. He laughed at the mild amusement.

As Jackson turned in a circle, he studied his surroundings. The private loading dock was empty except for the handful of soldiers, and fuel workers carrying a large hose and connectors to the body of the ship. The smell of fuel and cleaning fluid was faint in the air, common in such places. He shifted his weight, causing the disc to drift away from the Federation transport ship. It wasn't enough to make an escape, but it still amused him to make the soldiers chase after him to turn him around.

"I don't get it." Dodson looked up at him as he tugged Jackson's arm to steer him back toward the ship. "Are you like some kind of spy or something?"

Jackson kept his eyes forward.

"What did you do?" Dodson insisted. "Why do they want you so badly?"

Jackson didn't answer. Hydock, Aikens, and another man he didn't see the nametag of, sat on a cargo box. Their laughter rose and fell. He couldn't hear what they said, but the blustering tones reminded him of when he'd been in the same position—a soldier on duty.

"Where were you hiding on the ship?" the soldier kept prodding.

Jackson gave an audible sigh to show he was bored with the line of questioning and had no intention of participating.

"You can tell me who you are, or I can hold those friends of yours for lying to Federation soldiers," Dodson threatened.

"No, you can't. We're on an off-planet fueling dock, and on a ship that is not part of the Federation Alliance," Jackson dismissed. "We can lie to you all we want, and I don't have to answer your questions. The only reason you were let on board is because you threatened the docking lot authorities and they forced the captain's hand, but if you try to arrest a non-Alliance crew outside of Federation territory..." He purposefully let his words trail off. There was no need to point out that such an act would cause an intergalactic incident. Raiding and beating up a bunch of pirates was one thing, but an official arrest quite another.

"And we don't have to feed you on this trip. We'll see if you're so smug when we turn you in," Dodson grumbled. He kicked the disc and Jackson went floating across the private docking lot from him toward where the transport ship was docked.

As he turned, he saw Raisa standing in the entryway. She swatted at someone hiding on the other side of the wall. The fuel workers finished and carried their hoses to store them along the far wall of the private fueling area.

Jackson frowned. He shook his head once, trying to get Raisa to go back. If she saw the gesture, she didn't let on.

Raisa crossed the private fueling dock carrying a small container in her hands. She glanced up at him, and though her eyes lingered, she didn't acknowledge him otherwise. Jackson narrowed his gaze, glaring at her in hopes she'd turned around.

"Stop," Dodson warned at her approach.

"I'm looking for the two men who saved my life," Raisa said. Jackson frowned at the tone. It didn't sound like her, instead it was light and airy. She smiled and before Dodson could answer, she said, "There's one of them."

The leader of the fuel workers waved them away from the ship and off the docks, leaving Jackson and Raisa alone with the soldiers. Raisa continued forward, seemingly unconcerned with the fact she was surrounded by armed men. Hydock instantly straightening at her approach. Jackson leaned, trying to force the disc to move toward the conversation.

"This is an Old Earth recipe, very rare but delicious," Raisa said, lifting the top of the container and holding it out. "I will never be able to repay you for what you did."

"Just doing what I've been trained to do." Hydock puffed out his chest. He reached into the container and took out a cylindrical tan pastry. Lang and Berger walked off the transport to see what was happening.

Raisa offered them to the others, making small talk as they tried the food.

"Where are you going?" Dodson stopped Jackson from drifting toward Raisa. "Prisoners get rations, not treats."

"Take one." Raisa held the container to Dodson with a big smile. She glanced up at Jackson. He arched a brow. Did she think bribing the men with desserts would help his case?

Hydock came forward for a second helping.

Raisa tilted her head, watching the scarred man eat. "For Rick."

"What?" Hydock slurred the word. Lang stumbled into Berger, who in turn grabbed Aikens' leg for support as he fell. The weight of Berger's fall pulled Aikens from his perch on the cargo box and all three men collapsed on the floor. Lang moaned, trying to stand, but his knees gave, and he ended up on the ground.

Jackson tried pulling his wrists apart but was

unable to. Dodson spat the food from his mouth. Raisa dropped the container and gave a sharp whistle.

Dodson lurched for Raisa. "What did you do?"

She jumped back. Rick, Dev, and Lochlann ran into the private fuel dock to help Raisa. Dodson swung his arm to grab her and she jerked out of his reach again. The soldier tried a few more times, each attempt becoming weaker until he fell to his knees, and then forward onto the ground.

"You win that bet, baby cakes," Rick said as he approached. A dark bruise had formed beneath his eye and down his cheek. He looked to be heavily armed, as if he'd expected to have to fight his way off the fuel dock. "You took them down without throwing a punch."

"You let her come out here alone?" Jackson demanded from his prisoner platform.

"She had the best plan," Lochlann answered. "And it worked."

"We had few options," Dev said, his tone matter-of-fact. "And if I've learned one thing, it's not to underestimate the skills of a woman."

"You're welcome," Raisa added.

"None of you should be here," Jackson said. "It's too dangerous."

"Shut your black hole," Rick said, grinning. "You know you're happy to see me."

The man was right. He was happy to see them. Jackson would never admit that to Rick.

"You would have come for us." Dev crossed to the unconscious soldiers. He lifted them from the ground and sat them against the cargo crate in a more humane position. He then began searching their pockets.

"What did you give them?" Jackson asked Raisa.

"A little combination I came across by accident when creating a cream recipe." Raisa chuckled. "For obvious reasons, the company didn't preset it into the food simulators. If people realized half the things those units could be programmed to do, simulators would be reclassified as weapons."

"Are they dead?" Jackson asked.

"They'll be fine," Raisa assured him. "They'll sleep and wake up with bad gut aches and the need to go to the restroom."

"Serves them right, after the beating they gave me," Rick mumbled. Raisa nodded in agreement.

"And Blue?" Jackson asked, pointing a shackled hand toward the body.

"These guys," she gestured toward the sleeping soldiers, "came in at the last minute, shot a blaster and then claimed to be heroes. The blaster didn't appear to have an effect on her. I think she poisoned herself when I crushed her teeth with a wrench." Raisa turned her eyes down and frowned. "There must be some kind of venom in her bite. She got hold of Lucien. He's in the medical booth. He's stabilized, but he's looking pretty rough. Viktor refuses to leave his side."

"Why were you close enough to hit her in the teeth?" Jackson automatically tried to pull free. Again, it didn't work. He glanced at Dev to see if he'd found the keys yet. The man was still checking pockets. "I told you to stay where it was safe."

Raisa arched a brow and crossed her arms over her chest. Damn, she looked sexy when she was defiant. "Did you seriously think Alexis and I would hide in a bedroom when everyone else was in danger? It was bad enough we were forced to wait in the secret room."

Jackson understood the feeling. Staying in the secret chamber had seemed like a good plan at the time. That was before everything went sideways. It might have worked too, except that it hadn't. The Federation had poked around longer than expected. The medical chair attacked Raisa. Jackson gave the order to wake up Blue.

"We don't know if she is contagious." Jackson nodded at the body.

"They sealed Blue in a sterile bag. Alexis has been trying to process the information she heard from the recording. She thinks by cure, he meant he stopped her from spreading it to others. She and Violette are cleaning up the blood with sterilizers from the ESC crates."

"I kind of like him like this," Rick interrupted. He leaned down, took hold of the hover disc, and spun Jackson. As Jackson turned in a circle, Rick skipped around him in the opposite direction while humming a playful tune.

"Rick," Jackson warned.

Rick laughed. "Anyone want to play pass the space cadet?"

Raisa stopped Jackson from spinning. She placed her hand on his waist and looked up at him. The contact made the ache inside him deepen. He wanted to hold her, feel her against him. "What happened? How did they capture you? Did they hurt you?"

"After I left you, I went to warn Dev and Lochlann about Blue. I heard a couple of soldiers in the hall and tried to avoid them when two more came from the cargo area. They cornered me from both directions." Jackson gazed down at Raisa, wanting desperately to pull her into his arms. "I should have just knocked them unconscious and been done with it, but instead I tried to warn them about Blue attacking the ship. They blasted me on the back of my head for the trouble. I woke on this prisoner transport disc with a killer headache. It's my fault for letting them get the jump on me."

"Found it." Dev held up the key to Jackson's manacles. It was a rectangular demagnetizer, which fit into tiny slots in the metal restraints. Dev pushed it into one cuff and then the other. The shackles dropped and he caught them with one hand before tossing them at Rick.

Rick stumbled under the weight as they hit his stomach. "Watch it, Red!"

Dev chuckled and slid the key into the belt and ankle restraints.

Jackson rubbed his wrists and jumped off the hover disc. The second his feet hit the floor, he grabbed Raisa and pulled her against him. He whispered in her ear, "I worried I might not see you again."

"You're not getting rid of me that easily. I'm starting to like this pirate lifestyle." Her nervous laugh contradicted that statement. "We should go."

"Can we keep this?" Rick asked.

Jackson turned around to see Rick floating on the hover disc, his arms spread wide and his weight shifted to make the disc move over the ground toward the exit.

Dev went to the stacked crates and lifted one off the top that was marked as food supplies purchased from the docking lot. He moved to follow Rick. At

Raisa's questioning look, he shrugged and said, "They stole from us first. Like we wouldn't notice things missing off the ship from their search. Plus, they disrespected my wife."

Lochlann also grabbed one of the crates. "And they took our cleaning droid. These supplies won't cover the cost of the damage they've done, but it will be a start."

"Let's get out of here before they wake up," Jackson said. "We need to be out of this airspace."

Raisa pushed away from him to gather the container with the pastries before returning to his side. "Too bad we can't take their ship. It's in much better shape than ours."

Jackson felt his breath catch when she used the word "ours."

"What's wrong? Is it your head?" Raisa reached to touch his face.

"I..." Jackson gazed into her eyes. "I want it to be ours."

Raisa glanced back. "The ship? I was joking. A few crates are one thing, but stealing a ship? We can't."

"Jackson, come," Dev ordered.

Jackson quickened his pace, urging Raisa to do so as well. "No, I mean, I want everything I have to be ours."

They ducked under the exit of the private dock.

Jackson touched the door scanner to close it and slid the door indicator to "private" to ensure no one disturbed the soldiers while they were unconscious.

Raisa pulled on his arm as she hurried to follow the others. They jogged down the corridor leading to their ship. He glanced over his shoulder several times to ensure they weren't followed. When they neared the ship, Dev was already inside and Lochlann was passing his cargo box to him through the hatch.

Raisa ran ahead as Lochlann and handed her food container to Dev before climbing in. Jackson followed, locking the hatch behind him. When he turned, Raisa was waiting for him. She wrapped her arms around his neck and said, "I love you, too."

Joy filled him, and he couldn't help the smile that spread across his features. "I didn't say that."

"Yeah, but you were stuttering around it, and I thought I'd save you the trouble of choking the words out." Raisa leaned up to kiss him. He loved her confidence, and her openness. She wasn't a woman to run away from how she felt.

"I love you," he stated clearly to prove the words weren't caught in his throat. Their mouths were close as they spoke. "I want everything from now on to be ours."

"I think you just want to get your hands on my molecular gastro-spectrometer," she teased.

Jackson reached behind her, grabbed her backside, and lifted her off the ground so that she pressed fully against him. "I can assure you. Your molecular gastro-spectrometer is not what I'm trying to get my hands on."

21

"What did you do to my toy?" Rick exclaimed as he tried scooping the disassembled hover disc into his arms.

Raisa sat on the floor of the engine room by Viktor's tools. She hadn't meant to work there, but once she started, she just kept going.

"Turns out it has some of the same technology as my molecular gastro-spectrometer." Raisa glanced up at the pilot and laughed at his stricken look. "Lochlann told me I could scavenge it for the repairs."

"Oh." He dropped the parts on the ground. "I suppose that's all right."

"Thanks," she drawled. "I'm glad you approve of me making space credits."

"So, hey, about that box I gave you," he said. "Any chance you remember where you put it?"

"I hid it in the ESC meal pack crate in the secret lab. It's buried toward the bottom." Raisa bit her lip as she tried to connect the small wires inside the unit. She didn't touch them as she threaded it with her hovering finger.

"You are a star." Rick clapped his hands.

"What's on the information discs in the box?" Raisa finally managed to slide the wire into place and took a deep breath.

"Something very valuable."

He didn't look like he would say more about it, so she didn't pry. "Aren't you supposed to be piloting the ship?"

"Violette's at the controls so I can eat," he answered.

"Then what are you doing in the engine room?" Raisa picked up a soldering wand, held it over the wire, and pushed a button. A current surged, welding it into place.

"Wasn't hungry," he admitted. "There's no one chasing us so it's not much fun flying the ship."

"Hand me that plate?" Raisa pointed toward the cover.

Rick leaned over and picked it up. "You and Jackson."

Raisa arched a brow, not sure where he was

going with his comment. Her hand dropped as she studied his face.

"You know about his curse, right?" Rick waved the plate, reminding her to take it from him. "I'm trying to figure out where you fit in."

Raisa reached for the cover plate. "What curse?"

"When we were on Lintian, an ancestral spirit cursed Lochlann, Dev, our old shipmate Evan, and Jackson and me. She said that the secret to our future happiness was hidden within the five Lintianese elements—metal, water, wood, earth and fire. The element holds the secret to our future happiness, but if we don't recognize it when it comes, we will lose it and be forever alone. Lochlann, Dev, and Evan found their matches. And now Jackson found his."

Raisa didn't believe in curses, but she could see that Rick did. "And you're wondering what element is left for you?"

"Nah." he waved a hand in dismissal. "Just making conversation."

Raisa could tell he was lying. "Then, conversationally, what elements do you think are taken?"

"Dev is fire. Obviously. Evan is probably earth, since Josselyn was imprisoned in stone. Or maybe water because she was on an ice planet." Rick lifted part of the disassembled hover disc and pretended to study it.

"That sounds like a story I might want to hear sometime." Raisa fitted the metal casing into place. "Hand me those screws?"

Rick sat on the floor and gathered the handful of screws laying in a pile. He handed her one. "Josselyn is Violette's sister. Actually, it's a long story."

"And Lochlann?" She aligned the screw and held her hand over it to force it to move into place.

"Metal. Alexis was filled with nanobots and is like half computer." Rick handed her another screw.

"So that means Jackson is either wood, water, or earth," Raisa concluded. "I'm not sure I can help you out. When we first met, he kept saying I needed a bath. Maybe that makes me water, since I had to make a water-based concoction to bathe with. Or earth because I was dirty and…" Raisa thought about clawing out of the shallow grave. She didn't like thinking about it. Things could have gone so much differently that day. If not for Jackson, the Dokka would have killed her. "Then again, I have an affinity for planets with trees and cooking by campfire, which is wood."

"Not that it matters," Rick said. He handed her another screw.

"Wood," Raisa told him. "I think you'd be wood."

He lifted his fist and dropped the rest of the screws in her offered hand. "You and Jackson."

Raisa nodded. "Me and Jackson."

"It's good." Rick nodded and gave her a playful grin as he stood. He whistled as he left the room. The pilot acted like nothing bothered him, but Raisa knew better. He cared deeply for his makeshift family. He'd taken a beating to secure their hiding place. He was one of the first to grab a weapon to go after Jackson when they'd learned the Federation had him.

"Rick bothering you?" Jackson appeared in the door and her whole world felt like it brightened. He leaned over her.

"No. We were just talking about the curse." Raisa pushed her hands into the floor to lift high enough to give him a quick kiss. "We were wondering what element you were."

"Ah, the curse." Jackson chuckled. "I think I'm fire, because that's what I feel when you're near me."

Raisa laughed. "I thought Dev was fire."

"That's a little obvious isn't it?" Jackson waved his hand in dismissal. "Did Rick tell you how we became cursed?"

"He said an ancestral spirit did it." Raisa

finished screwing the plate onto the molecular gastro-spectrometer.

"Did he say why Zhang An did it?"

Raisa shook her head in denial.

"Rick came on to her. She didn't appreciate his brand of humor. I remember him saying something about twisting her panties. To tell you the truth, half the time Rick says stuff, we don't know what he's going on about."

"Spirit, as in ghost, as in transparent person?" Raisa tried to picture Rick propositioning a ghost. Jackson nodded. "How exactly would that work?"

"I find it best not to think about it." Jackson offered his hand. He nodded at the molecular gastro-spectrometer. "Were you able to repair your machine?"

"We'll find out." Raisa wrapped her arms around Jackson's neck and lifted up on her toes. She gave a small groan. "I should have probably picked a better workbench. That metal floor is hard on the hips."

"You'll just have to let me massage them for you," Jackson offered, letting his hands glide down her sides. A tiny shiver worked over her, as it always did at his nearness.

"So, what have you been up to my darling?" Raisa asked, enjoying his closeness.

"Alexis decoded more of the message. From

what we can piece together, after their village came down with this mutating blood disease, Blue's husband built this ship while he tried to find a cure for her. Since she drank blood, he needed a supply. That's where the Kintok came in. He used the traveling sex ship to feed her. Tank-boy Greg must have been part of the cure process. That part's a little unclear. The cure kept her from being contagious but didn't change what she had turned into. He put her in stasis, and eventually, when none of his ideas worked, he locked up the lab and killed himself by jumping out of an airlock." Jackson sighed. "I don't know if I feel sorry for the doctor. I mean, he must have loved her greatly to go to all this trouble, but on the other hand, he funded a pleasure ship and probably syphoned blood from the clients."

"If you were to tell this story to anyone outside of this ship, they would think you wove a tale of fiction." Raisa let go of him and gestured down to the molecular gastro-spectrometer before rubbing one of his strong bicep muscles. "Would you mind carrying that to the dining hall?"

"I am yours to command." Jackson winked. He lifted the unit and waited for her to walk out of the engine room first. They left the hover disc parts on the floor by Viktor's toolbox.

She looked up at the lights. "I have to say I feel much better now that the ship has power. Though, I suppose I *should* say I feel better now that Blue's off the ship."

"Speaking of secret labs, we're going to see if we can sell any of the medicines. There has to be someone who would want that setup for something other than blood feeding. We could stand to make a lot of money if we tear it down and sell off the pieces."

"I don't know, having a secret chamber is kind of neat," she countered.

"We'll keep the chamber. We just don't need all the medical supplies as badly as we need space credits." Jackson followed her into the dining hall and set the device on a table.

"You realize, if I get this working," she patted the molecular gastro-spectrometer, "I can earn space credits. I still have a job. And, with this ship roaming the high skies, I can find food samples from all over. It's steady pay."

"I do not expect you to support me," Jackson said. "I will provide for you."

Raisa smiled. "That's incredibly sweet of you to say, but I like my job. I like figuring out the puzzle of how to make something others enjoy. I like helping to feed people their native foods and sharing those culinary adventures with others who may never have tasted Syog ale or stew from Palpaton."

"I've never had stew from Palpaton," Jackson

admitted.

"Don't. It's awful." Raisa chuckled. "And I don't recommend visiting with the people of Syog for too long. They have some rather aggressive customs that include kicking each other in the…" She glanced downward at his hips so he'd get her meaning.

"Oh, ow." He winced and his stomach tightened. "Thanks for the warning."

"How about we support each other?" Raisa loved the feel of being in his arms. She felt safe when he was near.

"It's a deal." Jackson cupped her cheek and gazed into her eyes. "You're one of us now."

"A pirate?" she chuckled at the very idea.

"Family," he corrected. "And, being one of us, you have a right to know what we're doing."

"What are we doing?" She placed her hand over his.

He let go of her and walked over to the food simulator. "I need to figure out why the Federation wants me."

Raisa felt as if a weight settled over her. She stared at his back as he lifted his hand to rest on top of the unit without programming a meal. She didn't like where this conversation was going. They had just come out of danger, and he was talking about finding it again. "How?"

"There is a general I used to report to named

Ogden. I'll find him and ask." Jackson pushed several buttons. "Until I clear this up, they're not going to stop looking for me. Their coming for me put everyone in danger, and after that rescue, I'm worried they're not going to be as friendly next time."

Raisa automatically watched his selection. "That is a high-carbohydrate-level dish. You really should program in something with vitamins."

He turned to eye her questioningly as the unit dinged. Without looking, he opened the door and reached in. He pulled out a plate full of noodles with a white sauce. "You knew what I was getting without looking?"

"I program the simulators for a living. I have most of the recipe codes memorized." Raisa shut the door and hit the buttons to materialize vegetables. When the unit dinged, she pulled out a steaming plate of green cubes and dumped them on top of the pasta. "There."

Jackson grinned. "I kind of like this you-taking-care-of-me thing."

"Well if you eat like that all the time, someone has to." She wasn't baited with his smile. Worry still filled her. "Do you have to face the Federation? Can't we keep flying? Can't we change the name of the ship? Or the manifest?"

"Or my face and name?" he added with a shake

of his head. "It's better I deal with this head on. We can't be looking over our shoulders all the time. We have important work to do."

"The repossessions Alexis was talking about." Raisa nodded. If the Larceny Casino was taking possession of people and selling them to cover debts the delinquent gamblers owed, they needed to be stopped.

"Yes." Jackson placed his plate on the table.

"What if they make you reenlist?" Raisa asked.

He didn't answer as he sat at the table.

"It's obvious you don't like talking about that time in your life, so I won't pry, but I can tell you don't want to go back to that." Raisa hated the distance she felt building between them. She wanted to go back to holding him and laughing, but their relationship was relatively new and there was so much they hadn't had time to learn about each other. She loved him. She knew that. When he was near she felt better, whole. The idea of losing this opportunity to be with him was devastating.

But was her desire and love enough to stop the forces of fate?

Was it enough to stop the Federation from taking him away from her?

Raisa wasn't naïve. She had traveled extensively and knew that, as good as the Federation could be, and as important as the organization was, they were also a giant superpower within the galaxies, and with that came politics and corruption.

"There is nothing to tell. The things that happen in battle are not stories anyone needs to hear. I find comfort in the fact I always did what was right. I never harmed an innocent person and I always did my duty." Jackson picked up a fork and stabbed the food a little too hard.

"That doesn't mean it wasn't a hardship. The things you must have seen." Raisa almost added, "the things you must have done," but stopped herself. She tried to place her hand on his shoulder in comfort, but he tensed so she let it drop to her side. She took a deep breath and moved toward the doorway to give him space.

"It's the nightmares after," he said quietly, stopping her departure.

Raisa turned to study him as he spoke. He didn't look at her and she didn't move as she waited for him to continue.

"Everyone I killed had done something bad, but even bad guys scream and plead when it is the end." Jackson took a small bite and then dropped his fork as if he'd lost his appetite. "That's not what I dream about though. I remember the things those bad guys had done—transporting women against their will, overtaking villages, and…" He took a deep breath and she stepped closer as his voice grew softer.

"Horrible things. The worst things you could imagine one being doing to another."

"Then it sounds like you have nothing to be sorry for," she said.

Green eyes lifted to meet hers. "It's what I *couldn't* do that I'm sorry for. There was a political diplomat visiting Trag Seven. My unit was supposed to clear the area of threats before she landed but we were told to stand down because the diplomat wasn't part of the Federation Alliance and Trag Seven was. The diplomat, her husband, and their twelve children were murdered, and all because their homeworld wasn't part of the Federation's plan. I'd traveled with the family. I knew them. They were good people who were trying to make life better. I could have stopped the attack. We knew there was danger. We were right there, on-world, and we were ordered to do nothing. It was then I realized that if I wanted to make a difference, it wouldn't be under the banner of politics but out in the galaxies. Out here is where my talents are best put to use. In the high skies, I don't have to wait for orders to do the right thing."

Raisa approached him slowly. She leaned against his shoulder and pulled his head against her stomach. She stood, holding him, not knowing what to say. She heard the pain in his voice, felt it in the tremble of his body.

"The others don't know." He wrapped his arms around her, keeping her next to him as she stroked his hair.

"I have no reason to tell them," she answered. "But you are a good man, Jackson. You have to forgive yourself. Worrying about a threat and knowing the future are two different things. What happened is the fault of the person who ended their lives. If you had been there, if you had seen it, I know you would have done something."

"Ew, Jackson, what are those green things on your plate?" Viktor entered. He wrinkled his nose and shook his head as he crossed to the food simulator.

Jackson released her. Even though she had heard the pain in his voice and felt him shake, when she looked at his face it was expressionless. He reached for his fork and took a mouthful of the food.

"They're call vitamins," Raisa said, keeping her tone light as she deflected the conversation to give Jackson time to collect his emotions. They might not show on his face, but she knew they were in there, churning around his tough demeanor. "And you're going to have some too."

Viktor pressed the buttons to materialize his meal. The simulator dinged, and he took out a large square base piled with meat and other unrecognizable toppings. It was not a recipe Raisa had programmed. He folded the base in half and lifted it like a sandwich. His eyes met hers defiantly as he took a bite.

"Keep it up and I'll program the simulator to give out nothing but healthy, enriched super paste."

Viktor gagged, nearly choking on his food. He swallowed hard. "You wouldn't."

Raisa crossed her arms over her chest.

Viktor reached for Jackson's plate and stole two of the green cubes. He popped them into his mouth and mumbled, "Mmm, so good." The expression on his face said he thought they were anything but.

"That's better." Raisa nodded in approval.

"I'm going to get out of here before you try to feed me anything else," Viktor said. He carried his folded food out of the dining hall.

"Hey," Raisa called after him, leaning into the corridor. "How's your brother?"

"He woke up for a few minutes earlier mumbling nonsense. The medical booth says he's getting better." Viktor did not look heartened by the information.

"That's a good sign," Raisa said.

"I suppose." Viktor walked down the corridor toward the medical booth, where he'd spent most of his time since the fueling dock.

When Raisa turned back to Jackson, he was

almost finished with his food, as if he'd shoveled it quickly into his mouth. "Want to help me test the molecular gastro-spectrometer?"

"How?"

"I'll put something from the simulator into it and see if it can correctly break it down to its molecular levels." Raisa knew her job sounded boring to those who were not scientifically enthusiastic. She didn't expect him to stick around for a demonstration. Most of the time people tried to make excuses and ran away from her when she started working.

"Yes," he answered, to her surprise. "I would like to see how you do what you do."

"Really?" She couldn't stop the word from passing over her lips.

"Of course." Jackson nodded. He stood, moving to look at the unit as if waiting for her to start. "You thought it important enough to risk your life stealing it back from the Dokka. I've been curious to see what this molecular gastro-spectrometer does."

Raisa smiled. "I promise, it's fascinating." She reached for the food simulator and disconnected the power supply so she could insert it into her machine. The molecular gastro-spectrometer instantly began to vibrate. It sounded louder than normal, but the indicator lights turned on. "Now hand me your plate. Let's see if we can break down what you just ate for dinner."

22

Jackson watched Raisa sleep on the bed next to him. He leaned up on an elbow to better see her. They'd moved to his quarters, a small room with a bed, decontaminator, and not much else. He'd never thought about a woman living in his room before. As a man alone in space, the area served him well. He didn't need much—a place to sleep, bathe, and do his morning exercise. However, he couldn't help but think she'd be more comfortable in fancier accommodations.

He wanted to give her everything.

He had little to give.

All he had was the way he felt.

All he had was hers.

Jackson stayed quiet, wanting to memorize the way she sighed and moved in her sleep. If he had no choice but to rejoin the military, he wouldn't expect her to wait for him. What else could the Federation want? He had done nothing that warranted them coming after him.

Jackson had always suspected that men like him did not get to be in love. Since a young age, he was trained for fighting. Relationships failed when a partner didn't know where a soldier was, or if they were even alive. Years could pass before contact was reestablished.

The length of her naked body pressed into him. If he had his wish, it would be to lie like this forever. He wanted to marry her, to shout his commitment to the universes. None of that would be fair to her. In the scheme of a lifetime, they had not known each other long.

Jackson felt his heart breaking for all that he couldn't offer her.

Raisa's eyes fluttered open as she suppressed a yawn. An instant smile formed on her lips when she looked up at him. She touched his cheek. "You have that expression again."

"What expression?"

"The blank one. The less emotion you show, the more you have going on in that head of yours." She brushed the strands of his hair away from his face. "It took me a while, but I'm starting to read your moods. Soon you will have no secrets from me."

There was a teasing in her expression, but a thread of concern in her voice.

"I'll keep no secrets from you." Jackson had no idea what compelled him to make such a promise.

"Are you scared of being conscripted?" Her finger moved along the edge of his bottom lip.

Jackson shook his head in denial. "I'm not frightened by the job. It's something I know how to do."

"Are you thinking about Blue?"

"We made the only decision we could make, given the information we had. It would have been wrong to kill her without knowing. I do regret life was lost, but it could not have been predicted. I regret that I was not there to protect you when she attacked."

"Do you love me?" She rubbed her finger against his bottom lip.

He lightly snapped his teeth at her finger, not biting too hard. "That is no secret."

She hummed softly and rolled onto her back to stretch her arms over her head. She had no shyness when it came to her nudity, not that she had reason to be shy. He found her perfect. When she finished, she turned to look at him, staying on her back. "Tell me what you were thinking about."

"You." Jackson dropped his arm so that his head rested beside her. He pulled her naked waist toward his body so he could hold her close. "I don't want to leave you."

She frowned. "Then don't."

"I may not have a choice."

At that, she pushed up from the bed and he regretfully let her go. Her naked back faced him. "You have a choice, Jackson. You don't have to face anyone. They can't force you back if you don't want to go."

"I won't risk the lives of my crew. I won't risk you." Jackson stayed on the bed. She gestured her hand across the metal drawer in the wall, opening it to grab a clean shirt. Since it was one of his, it hung loose on her body. "You're angry with me."

When she turned to face him, she didn't look mad. "No. I'm trying to think of what I should say to you."

"You don't have to choose careful words with me. Say what you are thinking." Jackson sat up. The covers hid his hips and legs from view.

"On one hand, I respect your need to protect the people you care about. On the other, I don't want you to meet with the general. There has to be another way to find out why they want you." She ran her hands through her hair, pulling it off her neck and holding the locks on top of her head. "That Federation handheld I repaired. Maybe we can link it to the main system somehow. Alexis can find out how and I can build the machine to make it happen. That way you don't—"

"It needs to be directly ported to a base unit and then biometrics for the user are scanned," Jackson interrupted. "It's designed that way for security reasons to prevent the very thing you're talking about."

He'd talked to Lochlann about it. Rick already steered the ship toward a port near a military base. Arrangements had been made to keep Raisa safe if anything happened to him. He trusted Lochlann would keep his word in that regard.

When she didn't answer, he stood and pulled her against him. "Even if I am not here, you have a place on this ship for as long as you want it."

"Don't talk like that." She struggled against him, but the effort was weak, and he knew she wasn't really trying to get away.

"Power is restored to this ship for now, but it's only a matter of time before something else goes wrong. We can't afford to be looking over our shoulders all the time. I have to take care of this. Best case scenario is I simply tell them I am not interested in their mission proposal and leave." Jackson cupped her face and forced her to look at him. "Raisa, tell me you understand."

Her lips pressed tightly together.

"I need to hear you understand," he insisted. "I

can't go out there today and do what I must if I'm worried about you."

"I under—wait, *today*?" This time she pushed him harder and he released her. "You're meeting General Ogden today? When were you going to share this little bit of news, Mr. I Have No Secrets?"

"Today?" He wanted to make her laugh. Too late, he realized his humor fell flat against her rising irritation.

"I'm coming with you." She crossed her arms over her chest. She was adorable standing defiantly with his shirt flowing around her body. "Don't try to talk me out of it."

"I'm not going to try to talk you out of it. I'm going to forbid it." He mimicked her stance. Though, something told him that his nakedness wasn't intimidating her.

She tossed back her head and laughed. Raisa opened another drawer and pulled out a pair of pants she'd borrowed from Violette. She slipped them on, hopping as she pulled the tighter material up her legs. Then, grabbing her boots, she carried them toward the door. She lifted her hand to leave, only to pause and turn back to face him.

"You know, Jackson, I was buried alive on a lawless black-market planet, faced the Dokka, found the secret lab, fixed this ship, fought Blue, saved your ass from the Federation soldiers, and not to mention the fact I've been on my own visiting alien worlds for damn near all my adult life. I'm not some delicate ray of sunlight that needs protection from the shadows. So, I'm going to let that I-forbid-you comment pass this one time, because I know you're doing it out of a place of caring, but rest assured it *will* be this one time. The next time you decide to go all Neanderthal on me, I'm not going to be so nice about it. I'm disembarking with you, and that's final."

With that, she left him staring after her.

Jackson started to follow her but then realized he was stepping naked into the corridor and turned back around to get dressed.

As much as he admired her spirit and knew her capable, her little speech irritated him. He was going to keep her safe whether she liked it or not. General Ogden was a paranoid sort, and for good reason. With the ops he'd been in charge of over the years, there were a lot of people who wanted him dead. The man was not to be taken lightly, and he wouldn't want a civilian on his base.

23

Jackson didn't want to leave while Raisa was upset with him, but there was little he could do about that now. The port near Ogden's base, Fortress Hold Sixty, wasn't welcoming. It sold overpriced fuel out of a rusty pump, offered cooked meals that looked as if they'd been pulled out of the sewage system, and was run by a Gelertan proprietor who didn't give the impression that he was interested in much beyond the handheld viewing screen adhered to the wall. The man's appearance seemed humanoid until he moved. His skin looked like a sack around gelatinous insides that rippled slightly. This caused his facial features to droop. His clothes were dirty, stained down the front with the same color as the food.

This was no place for a lady.

Jackson glanced around. A faded biohazard notice was posted on the wall. The print was unreadable.

This was no place for any humanoid.

"What can you get for this recipe?" Rick asked Raisa, pointing at a bucket of the sludgy food.

Raisa wrinkled her nose and whispered, "Arrested for cruelty and attempted murder."

Rick chuckled. Jackson frowned at them both. This wasn't an outing. He was waiting to make contact with someone who would take him to the base.

"Honestly, it's not worth many space credits," she continued, her voice low. "There has to be a population that wants to eat it, and I don't think Mr. Stinky over there counts as a population."

"You should get back on the ship," Jackson said, giving a meaningful look to Rick. Why he thought Rick would understand and listen to his silent plea was beyond him. The pilot simply grinned wider and placed his arm over Raisa's shoulders, as he redirected her toward the window overlooking the fuel dock where they were parked.

The dock looked like a thousand others Jackson had seen in his travels, only more rundown. He'd been there before, years ago. Rust and age had taken its toll on the metal structure he was now in, and the neglect spread over the cracked lot outside.

Tiny gray rodents could be seen nesting in corners of debris. The planet was one of many previously uninhabited locations that the Federation had laid claim to. The low pressure levels made the air feel thin, not enough to hamper breathing on the surface, but enough to be noticeable. The rocky landscape had few plants, and all of those were low to the ground. The planet designation was simply, Federation Hold Sixty.

Fortress Hold Sixty located on Federation Hold Sixty.

The Federation Military wasn't known for its creativity when it came to such things. Where they excelled was secrecy.

Jackson went to Raisa and unceremoniously lifted Rick's arm off her shoulders and replaced it with his own. She leaned into him but kept looking out of the window.

"How will he know you're here?" she asked. "I haven't seen anyone approaching."

"I have to do this alone." Jackson couldn't take his eyes off her. "You can't come on the base with me. It will go better if I'm alone. If you are there, they'll see how I feel about you. Until I know what is happening, I won't let them use you as leverage."

"Don't go," she whispered. "I'm scared you won't come back."

"We have to be practical now. If I don't return, I

don't want you to wait." The words hurt to say. The idea of her with anyone else caused a physical reaction inside his chest.

"Fine. I won't stay in here. I'll go back on the ship."

"No, I mean I don't want you to wait for me if I don't come back. It's not fair of me—*ouf!*" Jackson let out a surprised breath as she hit him in the gut.

"Don't ever say anything like that to me again," she warned. "I love you. That's not going away. So if you don't want me waiting around, get your ass back to me." She arched a brow expectantly. "Tell me you understand."

"Yes, I understand."

"Good. Now tell me you love me and get this over with. The sooner we are off this dock, the better." Raisa clasped his arm tight and lifted up to kiss him.

Jackson wanted to do as she commanded. He wanted it more than anything. When their lips parted, he said, "I love you."

She nodded. He saw tears in her eyes, even as she tried to act strong.

Jackson took a deep breath and walked toward the proprietor. The man glanced away from his viewing screen for all of two seconds before turning his attention back to the screen. A tiny image of two gelatinous woman wiggled in a way that could only be described as disturbing, yet the proprietor seemed to find it worth staring at.

"You're a pretty princess," Jackson stated.

Raisa made a small noise as if her voice was caught between a gasp and a laugh. She hit his arm. "Jackson, be serious."

The proprietor reached over and pushed a button before pointing up. He didn't look away from the screen.

Jackson glanced up to where a security orb lowered from the ceiling. He held up his hand in greeting, knowing the device sent his image to the base computer. He held still, letting it record his face. It would be all the introduction he needed. It blinked with green lights.

"What is that?" Raisa whispered.

"It's how the general knows I'm here." Jackson lowered his hand.

"Ah, because no one would ever call that man pretty," Raisa concluded, understanding the code.

"They'll send a transport soon." Jackson glanced to where Rick poked the tray of food with a stick-like object. "Rick, you need to get her back on the ship before my ride gets here."

Rick must have recognized the seriousness of his tone because for once, the man didn't have a smart-tass retort. "On it."

"I love you," Raisa said, as if she needed him to know. "I'll see you soon."

Jackson tried to smile.

Rick looped his arm into Raisa's. "Come on, baby cakes. Jackson knows what he's doing. Besides, if he doesn't come back, that just gives us an excuse to go after him. It'll be more fun than floating around space."

She looked back several times as Rick led her toward the spacecraft. All Jackson could manage was a nod.

24

Raisa watched the viewing screen in the cockpit as a transport came for Jackson. The cylindrical air carriage had two propellers on the top. The blades were contained with circular ring that turned them in whatever direction was needed to steer the transport. No one stepped out after it landed. She touched the screen, as if feeling the flat texture of his image could somehow connect her to him.

"He'll be fine," Rick said behind her.

She dropped her hand. "Then why am I so worried?"

"Do you really need me to answer that?" He sat down in his pilot's seat and kicked his feet up onto the console. "Jackson was practically raised by the Federation."

"What do you mean?" Raisa didn't take her eyes off the transport as it took Jackson away.

"The military training program coordinator found him in an orphanage. They put him into their program, pumped him full of vitamins and food paste, schooled him, trained him. I only know bits and pieces of the story, but if anyone could be called a super soldier, it's him."

When the transport went out of view, she turned to study Rick, half expecting him to be teasing.

"He didn't tell you?" Rick asked.

"We didn't discuss his childhood," she admitted. "He doesn't seem to like talking about the past, so I didn't pry. I knew he was trained. I didn't know it was for so long."

"Can't blame a man for that." Rick reached for the console and pushed a couple buttons, changing the view on the screen. It showed the distance where a small spot was disappearing. "I've heard about those programs. All work, no joy. They stick the children into barracks and bark orders at them."

"Rick," Lochlann said in warning as he joined them. "Those are Jackson's stories to tell."

"I'm not telling Jackson's story. I'm telling what I heard about how the Federation trains children to grow into soldiers in their orphanage camps." Rick busied himself pushing buttons again. This time he brought up the view of the fueling station.

"That's why he doesn't show emotion," Raisa said, not so much a realization as an acknowledgement. "But he feels it. I know he does. We shouldn't be here. He doesn't want to go back. The only reasons he's agreed is to stop the military from chasing us, from chasing *me* because I drugged those soldiers."

Lochlann gave a small laugh and nodded. "Yeah, that was awesome."

"Couldn't have happened to a nicer bunch of guys," Rick drawled sarcastically, touching his stomach where he'd been beaten. The medical booth had begun to heal him, but it was a long process, and it had been days since Lucien could be moved out of it long enough for Rick to use it.

"This isn't right." Raisa clasped her hands in front of her. "I'm going after him."

"Whoa," Rick said, dropping his feet on the floor.

"Hold on," Lochlann said at the same time, moving to block the door. "We can't let you do that."

A low rumble sounded and the ship vibrated. For a stunned moment, they looked at each other.

"What was that?" Lochlann asked, moving closer to the console.

"I don't know. Checking sensors," Rick answered. "It came from outside the ship."

The view showed the storefront. Light flashed over the rundown metal structure. Raisa reached to push the button that would change the viewing screen.

The flashing light came from the direction of the transport. There had been some kind of explosion.

"Jackson," she whispered, running from the cockpit toward the outer hatch. She heard someone following her but didn't stop. Her heartbeat quickened, and she found it hard to breathe.

"What was that?" Dev appeared from his room.

Raisa's expression must have been enough answer because he gestured for her to keep going as he followed. She ran to the hatch along the belly of the ship, struggling as her hands shook to pull the lock so it would open. Dev and Lochlann appeared next to her.

Dev unlocked the door and hit the button to open it. He placed his arm in front of Raisa to keep her from going first as he jumped from the opening before the ladder could be extended to the ground. He looked up, holding out a hand so Raisa could use it as support as she hopped down. She placed her palm against his red one, lightly lacing their fingers as she used his strength for support and jumped from the ship. Lochlann landed behind her.

The flashing lights had subsided, but she saw

black smoke filtering up into the sky. The distance was too far to run.

Raisa turned to the fueling dock store. She pushed her way inside to find the Gelertan man standing near the dirty window looking at the distance. He appeared unconcerned.

"You're pretty," Raisa said, her tone hard. "Get me a transport to the base."

The man looked at her and snorted. The gesture sent a ripple down his chin and neck.

Lochlann and Dev entered the store.

"You're a princess," Raisa insisted. "A pretty princess."

"Raisa?" Lochlann asked.

"Blast it," Raisa swore. "I'll push the button myself."

She made a move to go behind the counter where she'd seen the smelly man push the button for the security orb. The Gelertan moved with surprising speed as he jiggled past her. He slid his body between her and the button and reached up to grab her by the neck. Squishy flesh compressed against her, molding around her chin to smother her mouth and nose. She tried to claw the skin around her face, fighting to breathe as she became lightheaded.

Just as suddenly as it started, it stopped. The man released her, and she gasped for breath. Dev stood with a blaster pistol pointed at the man's head.

"Transport," Dev stated, not lowering his weapon.

The man reached to the side and fumbled for the button. The security orb came down and Raisa went before it. After scanning Raisa's face, it blinked red, not recognizing her.

"Move." Dev ordered the man to walk in front of the scanner. The Gelertan appeared frightened by Dev and did as he was told. The unit recognized the proprietor and blinked green.

"Is that it? Will a transport come?" Raisa asked the man.

He acted as if he wasn't going to answer, but one glance at Dev had him nodding.

Raisa rushed to the window and watched for their transport. She tapped her fingers against the glass in her agitation, leaving dotted smudges behind. Smoke still drifted over the landscape. It felt like the air carriage took a long time before it appeared in the distance.

"It's here," Raisa said.

"Stay, or I'll come back," Dev warned the proprietor, his tone lower than she knew it to normally be.

"We need to be careful," Lochlann said as he

passed her a blaster. "We don't know what kind of greeting we'll get."

Neither man had tried to convince her to stay behind. For that, she was grateful. Nothing about this day felt right. Something had nagged at her since she'd opened her eyes. At first, she tried to tell herself it was worry, but it was more than that. Her eyes turned toward the smoke. The urge to cry welled up inside her, overtaken only with the impulse to run.

She ran to meet the transport but it drifted past her and she had to turn around. Her hair blew around her head as she neared it. Lochlann made a series of gestures toward their ship, most likely a message to Rick who watched from within.

"I shouldn't have let him go," Raisa said, not thinking anyone would hear her.

"Do you think you could have commanded him otherwise?" Dev asked her.

Raisa shook her head. "No. Just as he couldn't command me to stay on the ship when we landed today."

"Jackson is a survivor. We have fought in many simulated battles together in the VR. He knows what he is doing." Dev patted her shoulder. The gesture was a little awkward.

The air carriage stopped, and the door opened.

Dev held out his arm to keep her back as he looked inside before stepping in. Raisa and Lochlann followed him. There were bench seats curving around the sides that didn't have a door. They each sat against one wall. Raisa hit her hand against the door scanner, trying to make it close. Everything seemed to move too slowly. The windows were glass so she could see the countryside as they moved. There wasn't much to look at and the angle made it impossible to see the smoke. The carriage wasn't meant to be a tactical vehicle and so there wasn't much in its programming past moving from one point to another and back again.

"Do you smell that?" Lochlann asked. His eyes shifted to gold and she gasped in surprise.

"Dragonshifter," Dev stated.

Raisa nodded. "Of course."

"We're close to the fire." Lochlann touched the door scanner. It didn't open. A ripple moved over his body. Brown armor covered his flesh as he shifted. A ridge formed along his forehead and grew down to cover his nose. Talons extended from his hands.

Raisa made a small noise of surprise to see the change. She had never suspected.

Lochlann growled, showing fangs as he kicked at the carriage door. It dented at the impact and he did it again. The door flew off the moving carriage, crashing to the ground as they left it behind. Dev grabbed the door frame and leaned out of the opening. The carriage alarm began to beep in warning and she felt them slowing.

"We're near the base," Dev said. "Have your weapons ready but out of sight."

Dev jumped out before the carriage stopped. Raisa made sure her blaster wasn't on and tucked it into her pants under her shirt. She looked at the ground lurching past and leapt. Her feet stumbled, and she was flung forward. She landed on her shoulder and pain shot over her as her body rolled several times in the dirt.

"Come." Dev reached his hand down to pull her to her feet. The word sounded like a command.

Raisa nodded and tried to ignore the pain as she jogged after him. Seeing Dev pull out his blaster, she did the same. The circular dome of the base was near but she didn't see any movement coming from there. Lochlann apparently had landed on his feet and hurried toward the smoking transport. It was clear the carriage had exploded. Pieces of debris were littered over the ground, and the base of the unit was covered in flames.

"Do you see him?" Raisa yelled. "Jackson?"

Dev motioned her to be quiet. He came to a stop near the main wreckage and tilted his head as if listening. Lochlann stayed in shifted form as he ran around the area to check the surrounding landscape.

"I don't hear him." Dev went toward the fire. Raisa tried to follow but the heat blasted her and she stumbled back. "He's not here."

Raisa turned her attention to the base. The solid metal dome had been butted up against several large boulders, though they were hardly strategic enough to provide protection. The air carriage had drifted to a stop several feet ahead of them.

Lochlann joined them. He had not drawn a weapon in his search. "I found footprints leading toward the base." He pointed at the ground.

Dev started to run for the base but skidded to a stop as the entrance began to open. He tucked the hand with the weapon behind his leg to hide it from view and turned his body so it looked less unnatural. He walked forward slowly, prompting Raisa and Lochlann to do the same.

"Your name is Violette Craven Stephans en Dehauberkelsain en Thoraxian en Yyrtolzx Devekin," Dev told Raisa. "You're my wife, and your father was General Jack Stephans, who commanded the Rifflen base until his death. You don't like to talk about it."

"When did Violette officially change her name?" Lochlann asked in surprise.

"She and Lucien were bored. They added my

name to hers on official military paperwork because they thought it would be funny to watch people pronounce it," Dev said. "I offered to take her name, but she said she wanted mine."

"But, why would I need—" Raisa tried to protest.

"Raisa drugged Federation soldiers to free Jackson. Violette is a beloved military daughter," Lochlann interrupted her protest. He had shifted back into his human form. All traces of the dragon were gone. "We'll just hope Violette's image isn't in their system."

"It's not," Dev said. "I had Alexis remove it when she hacked into their system looking for the Larceny Casino information."

"She didn't tell—" Lochlann began.

"Now is not the time," Dev put forth. He nodded toward where soldiers came out with drawn weapons. "Time to play nice."

Lochlann signed heavily as if annoyed by what Dev revealed. He clearly didn't like the idea of his wife hacking into protected databases with her computer brain. Stepping forward, he led the way toward the base. Lochlann did not pull the blaster from his hip. Raisa again hid her weapon under her shirt. Dev kept his drawn and walked to the side as if ready to draw fire away from them.

"State your names," one of the men ordered.

"Captain Lochlann of the Draig," Lochlann answered before pointing at Dev, "Salebinaben Johobik en Dehauberkelsain en Thoraxian en Yyrtolzx Devekin," then at Raisa, "Violette Craven Stephans en Dehauberkelsain en Thoraxian en Yyrtolzx Devekin."

"State your business," the man continued.

"There was an explosion. We came to help but it doesn't look like there were any people on board," Lochlann said. His voice was calm and diplomatic, as he gave them no reason for aggression.

"The medic teams already swept the area. Is the traveler with you?" the soldier asked.

"Yes," Raisa answered. Both men looked at her.

"Jackson Burke," Lochlann added. "He's with us."

The soldier conferred with his comrades before lowering his weapon and waving them forward. He motioned at Lochlann's hip. "Going to need that."

Lochlann frowned but handed him the weapon.

"Yours too." The man pointed at Dev's hand. Dev gave the blaster to the man.

The man looked her over, and she lifted her hands to show she didn't hold anything. No one asked for her weapon so Raisa said nothing. Her baggy shirt must have covered the fact she wore one. They motioned for the three of them to follow. The man guarding the entrance stayed behind as two soldiers led the way into the base—one with dark hair walked ahead of them, the other with gray fell behind. Lochlann and Dev flanked her sides.

"Is he injured?" Raisa asked.

The men didn't answer.

"Are you taking us to see him?" she insisted.

"Everyone who comes to the base must first meet with General Ogden," the dark-haired soldier answered.

The gray-haired man didn't speak. Raisa didn't like the idea of an armed man behind them and kept looking at him. Whereas his companion kept glancing back at the visitors in curiosity, Gray kept his eyes focused forward.

She glanced at Dev and then Lochlann. Lochlann met her eyes briefly before darting his gaze forward as if to tell her to stop turning around. They acted like this kind of thing happened every day. Raisa had never found herself in the position of being escorted onto a military base by an armed guard under a false identity while smuggling a weapon. Her heart hammered violently, and her stomach churned. Her hand trembled and she drew it forward, balling it into a tight fist.

The Federation base didn't look like anything special. Metal rivets lined the main corridor that branched off into smaller halls to each side at regular intervals. Rows of doors looked to be barracks. The smell of food greeted them before they finally reached what must have been the center, as the ceiling peaked overhead. The rounded curve sheltered those within. Grated walkways crossed overhead at various levels, creating a star pattern when viewed from directly below.

"Keep moving," Gray ordered.

They were led past long tables set up for dining. She tried not to breathe through her nose as the food smell made her nauseous. Where was Jackson?

After leaving the center and moving toward another corridor, they finally stopped before a metal door. Nothing made it stand out from the rows of doors she'd seen on the way there, except the number two had been painted in the center.

The dark-haired soldier leaned his face next to a biometric scanner. The door clicked and opened on its own. He gestured them in. "Go on."

As they crossed the barrier, she wanted to ask Lochlann and Dev if this treatment was normal. It was one thing to confront corrupt soldiers on a fueling dock, quite another to walk into a base with no escape. Still, Jackson was in there somewhere, and that one thought gave her courage.

A man in a tan cotton tunic sat behind a desk. A thick brown stripe ran down his arm, signifying his rank as general. Wrinkles were carved into his features, as if the stern expression on his face had become permanently embedded. At their entrance, he swiped his hand through a holographic screen and it disappeared.

He gave a heavy sigh before standing. A slot opened on his desk and he reached in to pull out a packet. He slipped it into a pocket on his loose pants. The material matched his tunic, down to the side stripes along the legs. The shirt fell to his knees. "I am General Ogden. This is my base. You do not belong on it."

Dev crossed his arms over his chest as if daring the man to attempt to remove him.

"We're here to pick up a friend who is former military, Jackson Burke. If you'll direct us to him, we'll be on our way," Lochlann said.

"That is not possible," General Odgen said. "I'll have you escorted to the fueling lot so you can return to your ship."

"We're not leaving without him," Raisa insisted.

"You're not leaving with him," the general returned.

"Then I guess we're not leaving." She placed her hand defiantly on her hips. "You can take me to him now."

The general raised a brow at her command.

Raisa felt all her nervous energy building. She focused on a rivet on the wall. It took a lot of concentration, but she managed to force the rivet out of its hole. It clanked on the floor, drawing everyone's attention.

"I want to see Jackson," Raisa demanded. "Or I'll bring this whole place down."

It was a lie. She couldn't cave in the base if she wanted to. Rivets were hard if not impossible in some cases. Bolts and screws with threads were much easier.

"How would your father feel about this?" the general asked. He didn't look frightened by the threat.

"Jackson is a decorated soldier," Dev stated, "perhaps you should ask him if he wants to see us. It would be a matter of respect for the years he gave."

That apparently was an argument the general understood. He considered the words for a moment and then nodded. "Follow me."

Before leading them anywhere, though, the general went and picked up the rivet off the floor. He held it out to Raisa. She slowly took it.

"Threats don't suit you. You aren't the type to bring down a base and kill everyone within. That takes a certain kind of creature, and your eyes give your humanity away. You can also keep the weapon at your waist if it makes you feel better." The general walked out of his office to the corridor.

Lochlann and Dev both gave her strange looks.

"Do you know the trouble you could have

brought on yourself?" Lochlann asked under his breath so he wasn't overheard. "What were you thinking?"

"That I'm not leaving here without Jackson," she answered. "You two weren't saying anything."

"We were biding our time," Lochlann defended.

"Well, I'm new to this adventure thing," she whispered. Raisa frowned as Dev gestured that they should follow the general.

25

Jackson sat on the edge of the bed, staring at his reflection on the plastic wall. His image was transparent, more ghostlike than solid. He gave no expression, made little movements.

The box that made up his new quarters had lowered from above, locking him in without a door. He knew that poisonous fumes could come down the top shaft just as easily as oxygen. The cube made an effective prison hold. Beyond the plastic was a plain metal room. A chair looked like it had been sitting in the corner collecting dust since the base was first built.

Out of all the outcomes, he had not expected this. Arrested for a crime he did not commit. He would have bet his life that the Federation wanted him to reenlist. Instead, his arrival had caused an emergency fugitive warning. His air carriage had been attacked by the base soldiers who thought to catch him off guard while he was trapped in a carriage. After he leapt from the explosion, he'd been taken into custody. It was a smart play. Not many of them could have taken him on in a fair fight.

Jackson took a deep breath and held it.

Murder.

They accused him of murder.

Jackson tried to think of what he could have possibly done to make him a suspect because he knew he wasn't a murderer.

It was a good thing he came in. An enlistment, he could avoid. A murder charge was something else. And by helping him escape capture, the crew had committed a serious crime. *Raisa* had committed a serious crime.

At least she was safe back on the ship. Jackson could convince the general that they'd brought him in when they realized he was wanted. Since they had him, there wouldn't be a need to pursue the others.

Jackson has stared at his own eyes so long that the reflection began to blur. He sensed movement but didn't turn to look at the door beyond his cage. General Ogden appeared opposite his reflection. Jackson moved his eyes upward to meet the man's.

"Good to see you again, Jackson. I wish it was under better circumstances," Ogden said.

Jackson nodded. "General."

"You injured?" He nodded toward Jackson's arm.

Jackson glanced down, seeing blood on his ripped sleeve. The wound hurt, but not enough to cause alarm. Though they could both see the injury, he said, "No. sir."

"How long has it been?" Ogden leaned forward as if to study Jackson through the barrier but didn't touch the cube. The view was fairly clear.

"A long time." Jackson sighed. "Why does the Federation want me, sir? Who was I supposed to have murdered."

"That business on Trag Seven." Ogden's eyes narrowed and his lips pressed together. It was a slight gesture, but enough that Jackson knew he was irritated. "One of the daughters of Diplomat Peeple has raised a concern."

At that, Jackson stood and walked closer. "That's not possible, sir. All twelve of the children were killed. I read the report." Seeing the general's expression, he took a deep breath. "Which one survived?"

"Sharry, the youngest," the general said. "She's

taken after her mother and works as a diplomat for the Sevamp. They've signed on with the Federation Alliance, but she made it a condition that they punish all those she feels is responsible for the death of her family. They were supposed to have protection and she blames their bodyguards' lack of action as well as those who pulled the trigger."

"And I was chosen as the bodyguard who failed?" Jackson shook his head. This couldn't be happening.

"You are the only inactive member of the team. They had to give her someone." General Ogden didn't need to say more. The Sevamp was a big win for the Alliance, and since Jackson wasn't of value as a soldier anymore, he was expendable.

"After all I have done for the Federation," Jackson said.

"Yes, after all you have done." General Ogden frowned. "There is no loyalty anymore in this system we serve."

"I was ordered away. I wasn't even there when it happened," Jackson said. "The reports—"

"Have been lost," Ogden said. He sighed. "You have visitors. The woman was particularly insistent."

"Woman?" Jackson shook his head. No. By all the stars, it better not be Raisa.

"Violette Craven Stephans," Ogden said. "Do you want to see her?"

"Violette?" Jackson repeated in surprise. "Yeah." He nodded a couple times. "Yes."

"She has a big red fella with her, her Bevlon husband by the looks of him, and Lochlann of the Draig."

"Yes, I'll see them." Jackson sighed in relief. Thankfully Lochlann and Dev had kept Raisa away from this place. He knew he could depend on them to keep her safe.

The general crossed to the door and Jackson found himself walking along the cube to follow him. He reached the corner and stared at the entry.

Dev entered, followed by Lochlann. Jackson started to smile at them—but then stopped when he saw Raisa, not Violette.

Raisa hurried to him. "What's going on? Why is he in a cage?" She pressed her hand to the plastic wall and looked him over. "Why has he not had medical attention?"

Jackson shook his head, wishing he could convey all his thoughts to her with that one look.

Sadness and worry crossed her features as she leaned her forehead against the plastic. Her lips moved, and he saw her mouth, "What's happening?"

He shook his head again, unable to answer her.

"We sail under the banner of Var royalty. Jackson is a valuable member of our crew, and as such, is not subject to Federation law as we are not part of the Alliance," Lochlann stated. "Under what right do you lock him here?"

"Multiple murders." General Ogden moved to the door and shut it. When they couldn't be overheard, he said, "Wrongfully so."

"If you know he didn't do it, why is he locked up?" Raisa demanded. Her face turned from sad to angry. She placed her hands on her hips and faced the general. "Release him."

The general eyed Jackson. "Do you trust them?"

"As much as I trusted you," he answered.

"I didn't lock him up. When he contacted the base, I was not the one to process him," Ogden said. "By the time I was told he was on his way, one of my captains gave the command to apprehend the dangerous suspect. He's been reported. It's out of my hands. He'll be processed."

"No!" Raisa shouted. She turned to Jackson and placed her hand on the glass. Quieter, she said, "No."

Jackson placed his hand up against hers. Her fingers worked into the plastic. He wished that he could feel her. Murder of so many? Of a diplomat's family? There was only one sentence for a charge like this. Death.

He didn't want to die. He didn't want to leave Raisa. But at least he'd known her before the end. He tried to smile. His hand moved as if to cup her cheek. He didn't need to touch her skin to remember what she felt like.

"No," she insisted again, as if that word could change the course of events. "I told you not to come here."

"I met your father once," the general said. "General Stephans was a good man. He helped me when I needed it."

"No," Raisa mouthed to Jackson, shaking her head. Her expression pleaded with him to tell her what to do, only he couldn't. Moisture gathered in her eyes and she glanced up, as if trying to figure out how to free him. Louder, she said, "Jackson is innocent. Release him. You have no right."

"You're demanding like your father, too." Ogden chuckled. "Jackson, you could have done worse than a general's daughter. I'm sorry I assumed she was married to the Bevlon."

Jackson eyed Dev. The man gave a subtle indication that he was not about to correct anything the general was assuming. Maybe it was for the best they didn't know who Raisa was, in case the soldiers had reported what she'd done to them.

He didn't necessarily like lying to Odgen by

omission, but then again, the man had him locked up in a cell for murders he didn't commit.

A knock sounded on the door and the general shouted, "Enter."

A soldier in black appeared and handed an electronic clipboard to the general. Ogden read the screen and frowned. He pressed his thumb to the top of the device as if authorizing something and when he drew it away, blood dotted the tip of his finger.

"Send the report. I'll take care of this one myself. Leave us," Ogden ordered. The man nodded and quickly left. When he turned to Jackson, his expression was regretful. He took a deep breath and released it slowly. "I'm sorry, Jackson. It was an honor working with you."

Jackson lifted his chin. Tension rippled over him. He nodded at the general and turned to Raisa. "Dev, get her out of here."

"What?" Raisa demanded. "Why?"

"Dev," Jackson insisted, "please."

Dev placed his hand on her shoulder. She jerked away from him. "Why?" Her tone had become slightly shrill.

Jackson pressed against the plastic. "Look at me."

Raisa turned to him. Tears spilled down her cheeks and she shook her head. Her eyes begged him to make it all stop, to do something. She went to the barrier and put her hand against his.

Jackson wanted to say so much to her, wanted to express his feelings so she understood the depths of his emotions and how much he valued their time together. He knew that he didn't always show what he was feeling with his expressions, but she always seemed to know from the very beginning. He should tell her to find happiness.

A tear slipped from his eye and everything he felt boiled down to, "I love you."

"Jackson Burke," General Ogden stated. "You have been found guilty of murder in the Sevamp-Trag Seven classified incident. Your execution is to commence forthwith in accordance with Federation law."

"You can't do that! He has a right to be heard. He has a right to a trial," Raisa protested. She struck the side of the plastic as if to break him out.

"Not in classified military cases," Lochlann said. His entire body stiffened as he met Jackson's gaze. All he managed was a nod in his direction.

The general went to the wall and placed his hand on a scanner. Light flashed three times. The green glow colored Raisa's features. A control panel opened on the wall.

Dev growled and surged forward. He hit the cage as hard as he could. Blood smeared from his knuckles, but he didn't care as he hit it a second time. It did nothing.

"Release him," Lochlann ordered. He had shifted into dragon form and aimed a taloned hand for the general's throat.

"You will never make it out of this room if anything happens to me," General Ogden warned.

"Lochlann, don't, he's right," Jackson said. "He has a heart alarm. If you injure him, others will come. You will never fight your way off this base. They'll kill you. And, if you kill him, the room will lockdown and we'll all be poisoned. Don't forget your promise to me."

Lochlann glanced at Raisa and retracted his talons. His eyes burned yellow with anger. Jackson knew if she had not been there, the two men would have taken their chances in a fight.

Dev frowned at him. "This is not a proper end for a warrior."

"Thank you, friend." Jackson knew that was as close as Dev would come to affection. They had spent many hours together in battle and he knew Dev better than anyone.

"Dev," Jackson insisted. "Don't let her watch."

Dev placed both hands on Raisa's shoulders. She struggled against him, kicking and slapping to be free.

"Dev, don't listen! Fight them. Let me go. I don't care if they come. Let the soldiers come. Dev!"

The general pushed a button on the panel. Raisa struggled so hard she broke free from Dev. She ran at the general, dodging Lochlann as she slammed her elbow into the man's chest. The attack winded him and Odgen crashed into the wall. She kicked him, barely missing his groin.

The sickening sweet smell of poison misted over Jackson. He held his breath and looked up. It filtered in from the vent above.

Raisa punched the panel, breaking it. The general didn't move to stop her.

She ran to the cube and put her hands against the plastic. "Jackson, no! Don't leave me."

He stared at her as long as he could, until his lungs burned, and he had no choice but to breathe. He managed to say, "I love you," as the numbness took over his body. His knees gave out and he fell against the plastic and slid down.

Raisa followed him to the floor. "I love you. I love you! Jackson, no, don't leave me!"

He lost control of his body, falling to the side. His vision dimmed and the last thing he saw was Raisa screaming at him to stay.

N o.

Raisa stared at Jackson on the floor, and all will to move left her. Tears wet her face and her throat burned from screaming. She lay on the floor, facing him. His eyes had mostly closed but she could still see an edge of green. His parted lips didn't move.

She heard movement behind her but didn't care. Nothing mattered. She pressed her fingers to the cube.

"It's done. Send the death recording to command and then seal all files," the general said to someone.

"Jackson," she whispered, "open your eyes."

Raisa didn't move. The mist that had fogged the

inside of the cell was pulled up into the ventilation shaft like the lifting of fog.

Someone touched her shoulder and she pulled away.

"Raisa," Lochlann whispered. "Come on."

"I'm not leaving him." She didn't care if she ever stood again. "We should never have let him come here."

The plastic against her hand moved and the cage lifted. She scrambled forward to be next to him. Jackson's skin was clammy to the touch. She pulled him into her lap, struggling to move his lifeless weight.

"I'll arrange a transport to take you back to your ship," the general said. "You have no more business on this base."

Raisa caressed Jackson's cheek. Nothing felt real. Her entire world was numb. "I'm not leaving him."

"I'll have him transported to your ship so that you may make arrangements." General Ogden left.

"Raisa, I…" Lochlann's voice broke and he didn't continue.

"Why didn't you stop him?" Raisa demanded. She glared at Lochlann. "It was your job to protect your crew!"

The man looked as if she'd stabbed him. He inhaled a sharp breath.

"He was doing as Jackson made him promise to

do. Jackson wanted to protect you." Dev took a deep breath and looked as if he mentally braced himself to stay standing.

"You guys and your stupid honor!" Raisa started to sob. She rocked Jackson back and forth, not knowing how long they let her sit with him. Her sobs turned to whimpers, and she knew her heart would never love another. Life as she knew it was over. All that was left was a shell.

She didn't register anything happening around her. Voices sounded far away. The only way she managed to move was because two men lifted Jackson out of her arms, placed him in a dark container, and walked him off the base to a transport.

When Dev and Lochlann carried Jackson up the cargo loading bay of the ship, Alexis and Rick were there to greet them. Dev hit the button to close the door a little too hard.

"What did you scavenge?" Rick asked, looking at the container. "Anything fun?"

Raisa stepped out from behind Dev and went to where they had placed Jackson on the floor. She knelt beside the container and placed her head on it.

"What's going on?" Alexis asked, her tone nervous.

"Where's Jackson?" Rick demanded. "He is coming, isn't he? Or are we going in after him?"

No one answered him, but Raisa heard Rick swear under his breath.

"Oh, no," Alexis said softly. "Not that."

"Those bastards. Who are we killing?" Rick demanded.

"Raisa, I'm so—" Alexis' voice caught. "I'm so…"

"I'm blowing up that entire base," Rick swore.

Raisa opened her eyes in time to see Rick punch the metal wall. The angry thump vibrated through the cargo hold to the point she felt it where her cheek pressed to the container. She started to nod in agreement with him, but someone else punched something. She lifted her head as she felt the second vibration.

When she looked, everyone was staring at her. No one else had moved.

A loud bang vibrated the container yet again, and she gasped, jumping back in shock. She stared at the box, unsure she could trust her hearing. Raisa held her breath. Silence filled the cargo hold.

"Hey," a muffled shout came from within the container, followed by the sound of Jackson striking the side of it.

"Jackson?" Raisa yelled in disbelief. She grabbed

the lid and clawed at it in an effort to pry it open. "Jackson!"

Dev, Rick, and Lochlann joined her.

"Hold on, buddy," Rick shouted.

"Got it," Dev said as he pushed at the side of the container. The lid opened a few feet. She thrust Dev aside only to find Jackson's feet. His boot kicked the side of the container. It was the most beautiful sight she'd ever seen in her life.

"Get me out," came his muffled command. Several thuds sounded as if he tried to push the lid. Rick grabbed one side and pulled while Dev pushed. The lid made an awful grinding noise as it slid off.

"Jackson!" Raisa couldn't wait. She climbed into the container, putting her knees along his hips. She took hold of his face, feeling the warmth back in his skin. His green eyes focused on her and he gave her a small smile. "How…? I don't care. I don't care how."

Raisa pressed her mouth to his. She knew she murmured incoherently but she didn't care. The joy bubbling inside her could not be said in words.

Suddenly, she gasped and looked at Rick. "You need to fly us out of here. Now. Before they suspect anything."

"Gladly." Rick winked at Jackson and ran to the cockpit.

"Raisa." Jackson's voice was hoarse. "How did I get here?"

"It doesn't matter. You're here. You're alive. You're here." She kissed him again. "Never leave me again. Never leave me."

His hands lifted to her hips, but his hold felt weak.

"I don't know what happened, but we should get him in the medical booth," Alexis said. "Lucien is finally out of it."

Raisa nodded. She didn't want to let go of him, but she knew Alexis was right. They needed to make sure he was safe.

Dev reached in, scooped an arm behind Jackson's knees and the other behind his back, and lifted him in his arms.

"What? Dev?" Jackson tried to struggle as the man carried him.

"As Rick would say, shut your black hole," Dev stated.

Raisa gave a small laugh. Her body shook with fear, with relief, with amazement. She followed Dev as he strode through the corridor. Jackson's eyes closed and he dropped his head against Dev's shoulder.

"Hold on, boys and girls," Rick shouted over the intercom. "We're blasting off this rock."

The ship vibrated as the engines started. Dev

made it to the medical booth and locked Jackson inside. Alexis was already at the controls, typing in directions as she talked to herself. Raisa leaned against the edge of the booth and peered in at him. His eyes opened and met hers.

"I love you, too," she whispered, answering his words from the prison hold. "Jackson, I love you so much."

"He's going to be all right," Alexis said. "It's cleaning his blood. He's been dosed with some kind of tetrodotoxin."

"What is that?" Dev asked.

The ship jerked, and Rick began takeoff procedures. Raisa grabbed hold of the medical booth. She wasn't about to let Jackson out of her sight.

Alexis began mumbling to herself. "Tetrodotoxin. The anatomy of the Old Earth puffer fish. Irrelevant to the situation. Reexamine. Zombies. Dead walking."

Jackson winked at her and smiled as he mouthed, "Irrelevant to the situation."

To which Raisa silently said back to him, "Reexamine."

Two weeks had passed before Raisa was finally able to stop looking at Jackson like he was about to fall over. She barely slept as she watched him in the night. She monitored his food, always trying to feed him more. She walked with him around the ship. She knew she was hovering. She didn't care. Thankfully, Jackson didn't seem to mind.

"In the commotion, I forgot to give you your things back. The general handed them to me as we were leaving the base." Lochlann gave a folded bundle of papers to Jackson. They stood outside the dining room, where Raisa had tried to coax Jackson into another helping of the green vitamin cubes. He had humored her and ate them.

"Those aren't mine," Jackson dismissed.

"The general said they were," Lochlann insisted.

Jackson frowned, taking his arm from around Raisa's shoulders. She watched curiously as he opened the bundle. They were travel papers and identification chips. She frowned as she read the name. "Jackson Groober. I thought you said your name was Burke."

"It is. Groober was an alias on a mission a long time ago." Jackson scratched the back of his head before asking, "You said General Ogden sent these with you?"

"He said they were yours," Lochlann said.

"Was it a mistake?" Raisa questioned.

"No. Ogden was in charge of this mission. All relevant paperwork was turned back in to him when it was over. He must have kept them." Jackson gave a small laugh. "That sneaky bastard."

"What?" Raisa and Lochlann asked in unison.

"I wasn't quite sure if my living was on purpose or an accident." Jackson put the identification chip in his pocket and then folded the papers before slapping them against his palm. "He planned this."

"What?" They both asked again.

"General Ogden. He faked my death to make command think he'd carried out their orders, recorded your reactions to it as part of his proof, and gave me a new identity. Jackson Groober."

"That sneaky bastard." Raisa wasn't sure if she wanted to kiss the general or still kick him in his man-bits for what he'd put them through.

"Sneaky bastard, indeed," Lochlann laughed. "Well, here's to being off the Federation's radar, Security Officer Groober."

"Does it have to be Groober?" Raisa asked. "I mean, can't we pick a tougher-sounding name?"

"You don't like it?" Jackson pretended to frown.

"I'm just not sure I want to be Raisa Lovell Groober for the rest of my life." She was teasing of course. She didn't care what her name was as long as she was with him.

"Is that your way of asking me to marry you?" Jackson pulled her into his arms. His head lowered, inches away from kissing her.

"I'm not asking." Raisa grinned. "I find men like you do better when being commanded."

Jackson chuckled, nodding. "Yes, ma'am."

His lips met hers, and Lochlann cleared his throat. "Not to interrupt, but Rick asked to use the viewing screen in my quarters The power surges fried his. Apparently, we're all invited to join him."

Raisa shared a look with Jackson.

"Should we be worried?" Raisa asked.

"Probably," Lochlann answered.

Curious as to what Rick was up to, they followed Lochlann to the captain's quarters.

As they approached, Violette walked out of the room shaking her head. "Dev was right. I should have known better."

"I didn't actually think you'd show up," Rick yelled after her.

Against her better judgement, Raisa walked past the cage in the middle of the room. She saw the box that Rick had asked her to hide from the Federation and guard with her life. One of the information discs was missing.

"You have been a bad boy, Mr. Smith," a female voice said.

Raisa frowned and moved around the corner. The viewing screen was filled with a buxom woman puckering her lips and biting a finger. The style of her clothes was strange as she bent over to show a full view of her naked ass under her skirt.

"Oh!" Raisa lifted her arm to hide her eyes. "*That* is what you had me hiding from the Federation?"

"Worth it, right?" Rick grinned.

The woman onscreen made a funny noise, and Raisa grabbed Jackson's arm to pull him away from the viewing area. "You haven't heard the last of this, Rick."

"You can borrow it later," he offered.

"No. Just no. Get out," Lochlann ordered.

"But my viewing screen is broken and—" Rick protested.

"Take the discs with you or I'll break them," Lochlann warned.

"No, I'm going, don't hurt my Cindy."

They heard a scuffle as Raisa and Jackson rushed out of the captain's quarters.

"I can promise you one thing, Raisa Lovell Groober, life in space will never be dull." Jackson hooked his arm over her shoulders as he directed her back to their private room.

"I'm all right with dull, as long as you're safe." She grinned, slipping from under his arm to face him as she walked backwards. "But if you want an adventure, we can try to create chocolate with my molecular gastro-spectrometer. Whoever figures that one out is going to be rich."

"You're a wild one," he teased.

She grabbed him by his shirt and pulled him toward their room. "Oh, you have no idea, Mr. Smith."

Jackson laughed, letting her lead him wherever she wanted.

"You've been a very bad boy," she continued, pursing her lips.

Jackson swept her into his arms and carried her the rest of the way into the room. His lips met hers and she laughed as he kissed her. After all they had been through together, she knew they could face anything. Jackson was her forever.

The End

THE SERIES CONTINUES...

Space Lords Series
His Frost Maiden
His Fire Maiden
His Metal Maiden
His Earth Maiden
His Woodland Maiden

HIS WOODLAND MAIDEN

Space Pirate Rick Hayes flies the high skies searching for mischief. It looks like she finally found him.

From NY Times & USA TODAY Bestselling Author, Michelle M. Pillow, a space adventure romance!

Space pirate and all-around bad boy, Rick Hayes isn't looking to change his ways. He's one helluva pilot, has a crew he thinks of as family, and women seem to want his company. What more could a guy want? Life is too short to settle down, and he knows firsthand the less you care about, the less it hurts when you lose it. Too bad his logic doesn't always get through to his heart. When fate tempts him with a beautiful woman that appears to see through all of his defenses...

Well, actually, the frustrating star beam took him prisoner, hit him over the head, and stole his memories. Regardless of those few minor hiccups on the road to romance, Rick has to decide if love is worth the risk.

Chapter One Excerpt

Lin Yao Mines, Planet of Lintian

Rick Hayes couldn't remember most of the journey to the purple jade mines, but he remembered her. He didn't have a name for *her*. She hadn't given him one before hitting him over the head and taking him prisoner.

The smell of dank earth filled each breath. At least they'd put him on a portable chair and not the rocky ground. It wasn't luxury, but it was something. His eyes had long adjusted to the dim lights strung across the mine's ceiling. It cast the jagged edges of the stone walls into contrast. His hands worked against his ties. He knew very little about this planet and had no way of knowing what manner of creatures called Lintian home. So, when he escaped it should prove interesting.

Her, otherwise known as the dark-haired enchantress, had smiled at him while they were docked on Leinad's star port where they'd stopped for fuel. He knew the look of feminine invitation and assumed she wanted him to follow her as she left the bar. It was only after he pursued her into some kind of criminal meet-n-greet that he realized his assumption might have been wrong. Being a space pirate himself, Rick usually fit right into such questionable situations. This had not been one of those times.

Rick and his crew had been on their way to Qurilixen, the homeworld of their ship's captain. Prince (aka Captain) Jarek's family ruled half of the planet, so they were always treated like royalty when they visited—soft beds, endless food, drinking, and gaming. Unmated females were rare, so it did lack one thing. Still, a soft bed would be better than being trussed up like a human sacrifice.

"The bosses aren't going to like this," he heard one of the men whisper from an adjoining tunnel. The rest of the kidnappers hadn't given their names either. "This pirate doesn't factor into our plans. We should have killed him before leaving the star port."

Rick had been able to figure out he was being held by intergalactic drug traders. For the most part, his abductors had made it very clear they wanted to kill him. It was only the woman who'd kept him alive.

Rick tried to suppress his grin. Not surprising since he did have a way with the ladies.

Currently they were near some place called the Lin Yao Mines located in Singhai near the Shan Gung Din palace. The information meant little to him except where there was a civilization there would be a ship he could steal to escape the planet. Rick could fly pretty much anything.

His crew would come for him... if they knew where to look. Since he'd been unconscious when the enchantress' ship left the star port, he wasn't sure if his friends knew who'd taken him. That meant he was on his own until proven otherwise.

A series of loud thuds sounded from the tunnel. He craned his neck and tried to jerk his feet free from the binds. The drug dealing enchantress appeared in the yellowed light. Blue lines encased her dark eyes. Only, her gaze wasn't sparkling with mischief like he'd grown accustomed to seeing. She came to him in a panic.

"Change of plans," she whispered, digging in the pouch at her thigh only to pull out a syringe.

"Oh, hold on babycakes, there's no reason to do anything rash." Rick leaned away from her hand, not knowing what kind of threat was in the syringe. "We've come so far. No reason to resort to killing me now."

"I had planned on wiping your mind and leaving you on some remote fueling dock with a couple of hundred credits so your space pirate buddies could find you, but it looks like I'll have to do this our normal way."

"What do you mean our normal way? We have a normal way?" He pushed his feet against the floor, trying to move the chair and unable to get it to do more than rock back and forth.

"I know you won't remember this, but you need to stop following me, Rick. I hope this thought embeds deeply in your mind. If you see me, walk the other way. I can't keep saving you. This has to be the last time." She licked her lips.

"What are you talking—?"

The words were cut off as she pressed her mouth to his. She kissed him deeply, grasping the back of his head with one hand. It wasn't a sweet, testing kiss, but one from a woman who'd done this to him before. Surely, he'd remember such a thing. Her touch felt familiar. His body responded instantly, and he groaned, fighting against his ties.

A sharp jab pierced his thigh, but he hardly cared. When she pulled back, breathing as hard as he, Rick tried to follow her mouth to continue.

She put her hand to his lips to stop him and said, "You won't remember this, but I am sorry. Good luck."

Rick blinked hard. She threw the syringe down a dark crevice and turned toward the tunnel where her men were.

"Release him," a loud voice ordered. Rick detected a flash of red trimmed in gold as a man entered the cave. More was said, but the words became muffled as his vision darkened. He felt his body slumping forward but was too weak to stop it.

To find out more about Michelle's books visit
www.MichellePillow.com

ABOUT MICHELLE M. PILLOW

New York Times & *USA TODAY*
Bestselling Author

Michelle loves to travel and try new things, whether it's a paranormal investigation of an old Vaudeville Theatre or climbing Mayan temples in Belize. She believes life is an adventure fueled by copious amounts of coffee.

Newly relocated to the American South, Michelle is involved in various film and documentary projects with her talented director husband. She is mom to a fantastic artist. And she's managed by a dog and cat who make sure she's meeting her deadlines.

For the most part she can be found wearing pajama pants and working in her office. There may or may not be dancing. It's all part of the creative process.

Come say hello! Michelle loves talking with readers on social media!

www.MichellePillow.com

facebook.com/AuthorMichellePillow

twitter.com/michellepillow

instagram.com/michellempillow

bookbub.com/authors/michelle-m-pillow

goodreads.com/Michelle_Pillow

amazon.com/author/michellepillow

youtube.com/michellepillow

pinterest.com/michellepillow

MORE QURILIXEN WORLD BOOKS

Want to read the connected series?

Check out the first book in the connected series
installments.

Dragon Lords: Barbarian Prince
Lords of the Var®: The Savage King
Space Lords: His Frost Maiden
Captured by a Dragon-Shifter: Determined Prince
Galaxy Alien Mail Order Brides: Spark
Dynasty Lords: Seduction of the Phoenix
Qurilixen Lords: Dragon Prince

COMPLIMENTARY EXCERPTS

PERFECT PRINCE

BY MICHELLE M. PILLOW

Dragon Lords Series

A Perfect Escape...

Nadja Aleksander has everything she could ever want in life, except her freedom. Skipping out on her engagement, to a man her controlling father has chosen for her, Nadja books passage on the first spaceship she can find. Bound for a planet of primitive humanoid males, Nadja plans on finding a simple, hardworking man who will allow her to live out her days in total obscurity.

A Perfect Mistake...

Dragon-shifter Prince Olek is pleased with his refined and blushing bride. When she chooses him to be her life mate, appearing happy in her decision, his heart soars—until the next morning when his new princess wants nothing to do with him. Olek doesn't know what he's done to upset his alluring bride, but he is determined to reignite the hot sparks that burned the night they met.

Perfect Prince Excerpt

"Come, bride."

Again, she couldn't deny him, moving to dip under the green tent flap he held up for her. When she drew near him, she smelled the warm oil on his glistening skin. It mixed with the natural scent of him. She breathed deeply. This was as close as she had ever been to such an inadequately dressed man before.

She faltered in her movements, glancing up into his eyes. Before she knew what was happening, a strong hand was on her face, gently cupping her cheek. The touch was fire to her already flushed features. Her lips parted with a ragged, scared gasp. Olek took it as an invitation and dipped his head forward.

Nadja almost screamed when he tried to kiss her. Her first reaction was to run. Dodging under his arm, she darted inside the tent. Nadja froze mid-step as she looked around. The red earth floor was covered completely in soft furs. It cushioned her feet beneath her slippers. Below the center point of the pyramid was a high platform bed, which required a step to climb onto it. Silk hung down around the sides, stirring delicately in the torchlight like soft white clouds.

She should have run *out* of the tent, not in.

Spinning to do just that, she realized the only exit was still blocked. She was trapped. Olek grinned, though the look seemed baffled.

"I-I," she stuttered, not sure how to explain her rude behavior, or if she even should.

Olek let the flap fall shut behind him as he followed her inside. He resembled a stalking beast after his prey, relishing the anticipation of the hunt.

Nadja turned from him and was again met with the giant bed. She recoiled from it as if it was covered in poison. It occurred to her how intimate this night really could be. Stumbling back, she bumped into an incredibly hard chest.

She jolted in panic, scurrying away from the solid, warm muscles. Her eyes darted around, taking in the three corners of the enclosure. In the first, there was a bath drawn, the steaming water coming out of the basin. A sweet perfumed scent rose with it. Folded towels, bath oils, and rinses were neatly arranged at the side.

The next corner had a table full of chocolates, fruits and cream sauces. A bench with cushioned seats stretched along the side, resembling a couch. An earthen wine jug was set in the center. Feeling the heady consequences of the liquor she had drunk too much of at the feast, she turned away from the food.

The third corner, behind the bed, was harder to see from her position so she ignored it. Feeling rather than hearing Olek coming up behind her, she again panicked. Swirling to face him, she held up her arms and backed away. Her hands shook. This was not how she imagined being alone with a man would feel like. She always assumed it would be like reporting to one of the robot guards, or talking to a dignitary at some function she was forced to attend.

But Olek was half naked and smiling at her like he knew every thought in her head. Did he somehow realize she liked looking at his oiled chest, to the point where she made a conscious effort not to? Could he know that when his hand had briefly held hers, her nerves had tingled, were still tingling? That the idea of his kisses both excited and terrified her?

Merriment poured from his gaze and she blushed to see it. He held back, standing tall as Nadja studied him. Before she realized it, her eyes were traveling a seductive journey of discovery over his taut chest. Already his small nipples were hard buds. His flesh dipped in all the right places only to rise and swell with each of his shallow breaths. There was no fat on his chiseled form and she doubted they employed beauty services to remove fat cells on a planet like this. His body was all natural. She bit her bottom lip, absently chewing at it as she looked him over.

His broad shoulders carried his strong arms with ease. They were arms that could crush her if he so chose. The metal band on his biceps would have fit on top of her head like a crown. Looking closer, she saw that the jewelry was shaped like a dragon winding over flesh.

Nadja looked at his covered face. He did indeed appear bold and strong like a dragon.

"Are you pleased?" he asked confidently when she didn't move. Again, his smile was alluring and light. She could tell by the expression that this was a man who laughed often.

She blinked nervously, trying to erase the image of tight flesh burning into her memory. He took a step forward, moving as if to touch her.

"No," she commanded, her eyes narrowing. Her words stopped him. Her breathing deepened. "Just stay back a moment."

His head tilted to the side, waiting for her command.

Nadja took another deep breath, trying to control her undisciplined emotions and wild heartbeat.

"I don't think there is a need to do any of..." She swallowed nervously and looked at the bath and then the bed. Shivering, she tried to lift her hands to cross protectively over her chest and grew frustrated by the binding straps. With a frown, she tugged the belt off her arms. "I meant to say, I know the tradition of this night is to prove yourself a worthy mate by a display of your..."

As Olek arched a brow, she saw the shifting beneath his mask. His eyes dipped to focus on the way her breasts bounced with her jerking movements. She freed herself from the arm ties and left them to hang at her waist.

Swallowing over her embarrassment, she crossed her arms over her chest to break his gaze, and uttered, "Your prowess."

The grin widened over his amazingly firm lips. Those lips weren't fair. No man should look that delectable. Nadja made a small sound of distress before continuing. She knew he wanted her to choose him for her husband. It wasn't fair. He couldn't really speak until she granted him permission. The only way to grant him permission was to accept him as a husband. Hurting his feelings wasn't a great way to start off their possible life together, so she tried to speak carefully.

"I am telling you, there is no need for that. I am not concerned with…" Nadja felt like kicking herself. The words sounded weak and trembling. Normally she could speak with soft confidence, always reasonable and logical and well-phrased. Her voice came out in hot, breathless pants. What was he doing to her? Her body felt like it was on fire, like she needed to take off her clothes and jump into a snow drift. She started to sweat. Absently, she fanned her face, trying to concentrate. Forgetting where she had left off, she repeated, "I am not concerned with your prowess—*ah!*"

Olek boldly whipped his loincloth from his hips and dropped it to the fur-lined floor.

**To find out more about Michelle's books
visit www.MichellePillow.com**

LOVE POTIONS

WARLOCKS MACGREGOR SERIES

Michelle M. Pillow

Contemporary Paranormal Scottish Warlocks

A little magickal mischief never hurt anyone…

Erik MacGregor, from a clan of ancient Scottish warlocks, isn't looking for love. After centuries, it's not even a consideration…until he moves in next door to Lydia Barratt. It's clear that the shy beauty wants nothing to do with him, but he's drawn to her nonetheless and determined to win her over.

Lydia Barratt just wants to be left alone to grow flowers and make lotions in her old Victorian house. The last thing she needs is a demanding Scottish man meddling in her private life. Just because he's gorgeous and totally rocks a kilt doesn't mean she's going to fall for his seductive manner.

But Erik won't give up and just as Lydia let's her guard down, his sister decides to get involved. Her little love potion prank goes terribly wrong, making Lydia the target of his sudden embarrassingly obsessive behavior. They'll have to find a way to pull Erik out of the spell fast when it becomes clear that Lydia has more than a lovesick warlock to worry about. Evil lurks within the shadows and it plans to use Lydia, alive or dead, to take out Erik and his clan for good.

Love Potions Excerpt

"Ly-di-ah! I sit beneath your window, laaaass, singing 'cause I loooove your a—"

"For the love of St. Francis of Assisi, someone call a vet. There is an injured animal screaming in pain outside," Charlotte interrupted the flow of music in ill-humor.

Lydia lifted her forehead from the kitchen table. Her windows and doors were all locked, and yet Erik's endlessly verbose singing penetrated the barrier of glass and wood with ease.

Charlotte held her head and blinked heavily. Her red-rimmed eyes were filled with the all too poignant look of a hangover. She took a seat at the table and laid her head down. Her moan sounded something like, "I'm never moving again."

"You need fluids," Lydia prescribed, getting up to pour unsweetened herbal tea from the pitcher in the fridge. She'd mixed it especially for her friend. It was Gramma Annabelle's hangover recipe of willow bark, peppermint, carrot, and ginger. The old lady always had a fresh supply of it in the house while she was alive. Apparently, being a natural witch also meant in partaking in natural liquors. Annabelle had kept a steady supply of moonshine stashed in the basement. If the concert didn't stop soon she might try to find an old bottle.

"Ly-di-ah!"

"Omigod. Kill me," Charlotte moaned. "No. Kill him. Then kill me."

"Ly-di-ah!"

Erik had been singing for over an hour. At first, he'd tried to come inside. She'd not invited him and the barrier spell sent him sprawling back into the yard. He didn't seem to mind as he found a seat on some landscaping timbers and began his serenade. The last time she'd asked him to be quiet, he'd gotten louder and overly enthusiastic. In fact, she'd been too scared to pull back the curtains for a clearer look, but she was pretty sure he'd been dancing on her lawn, shaking his kilt.

"Omigod," Charlotte muttered, pushing up and

angrily going to a window. Then grimacing, she said, "Is he wearing a tux jacket with his kilt?"

"Don't let him see you," Lydia cried out in a panic. It was too late. The song began with renewed force.

"He's..." Charlotte frowned. "I think it's dancing."

Since the damage was done, Lydia joined Charlotte at the window. Erik grinned. He lifted his arms to the side and kicked his legs, bouncing around the yard like a kid on too much sugar. "Maybe it's a traditional Scottish dance?"

Both women tilted their heads in unison as his kilt kicked up to show his perfectly formed ass.

"He's not wearing..." Charlotte began.

"I know. He doesn't," Lydia answered. Damn, the man had a fine body. Too bad Malina's trick had turned him insane.

To learn more about Michelle's books visit:
www.MichellePillow.com

PLEASE LEAVE A REVIEW
THANK YOU FOR READING!

Please take a moment to share your thoughts by leaving a review.

Be sure to check out Michelle's other titles at

www.michellepillow.com